THE PARKER TWINS SERIES

6

SERIES

Race for the Secret Code

THE PARKER TWINS SERIES

6
THE PARKER TWINS SERIES

Race for the Secret Code

JEANETTE WINDLE

Kregel
Publications

Race for the Secret Code

Previously published as *Escape to Deer Island.*

© 1996, 2002 by Jeanette Windle

Published by Kregel Publications, a division of Kregel, Inc., P.O. Box 2607, Grand Rapids, MI 49501. For more information about Kregel Publications, visit our Web site: www.kregel.com.

Cover illustration: Patrick Kelley
Cover design: John M. Lucas

ISBN 0-8254-4144-7

Printed in the United States of America

1 2 3 4 5 / 06 05 04 03 02

I'M DROWNING

He was lost in the icy wet darkness! Somewhere out there, only a few hundred yards away, glowed the lights that could bring him to safety. And somewhere in the same black night loomed his enemies!

But where? Justin kicked desperately in the water, not only to stay afloat, but to bring warmth back to his body. Caught in the trough between the long ocean swells, he saw nothing but rough, dark waves tossing and splashing all around him.

It had seemed so easy! His enemies hadn't followed his desperate dive overboard. The swim to land would be long and cold, but he was strong. He could make it! *But which way to swim?* He couldn't linger long in these winter waters!

A wave lifted him high. It held for just a moment, then curled over lazily, washing him under water. He choked and gagged as he fought his way back to the surface. But he had glimpsed the distant city skyline. Gritting his teeth to keep them from chattering, he struck out for the shore.

His arms and legs ached with cold. The swells grew higher and rougher and though he swam with all his strength the shoreline lights drew no closer.

I've got to keep going! he told himself grimly. If he didn't make it to safety, his enemies would win. Unless the precious package tucked inside his jacket was returned safely, not only his family but the entire country would be in danger!

As Justin swam on, a slow feeling of warmth crept into his numbed limbs. He treaded water for a brief rest, letting swells lift and drop him in a sleepy rhythm. Why had he thought the waters so cold? This swim was almost pleasant—if only he wasn't so tired. His head drooped forward.

Wake up! Danger! He tried to ignore the screaming voice in his head. *You've got to keep moving!*

He forced himself into sluggish movement, scanning the night for light to guide him. But when he looked over his shoulder, he gasped in horror. A mountain of salt water curved slowly above him, the foam of its crest reaching ghostly white fingers toward the exhausted boy.

He had to move, but his arms and legs felt like lead. For an instant, he watched the wave hover above him. Then gravity won as thousands of pounds of salt water crashed down upon him.

With dull surprise, Justin realized—*I'm drowning!*

Chapter One

DEER ISLAND

"Psst, Jenny! I think someone's following us!"

Jenny peered through a magnifying glass set in the top of a long, wooden case. Underneath was an ordinary pin, its tiny head etched with the entire Lord's Prayer. "What did you say?" she said absently without glancing up.

Justin's voice rose a little. "I said, I think someone's following *us!*"

This time Jenny did look up. "Oh, Justin!" she wailed. "Not again."

Hands on her hips, she turned to survey the small trading post. Early November was long past tourist season on the Seattle waterfront, and Ye Olde Curiosity Shop, with souvenirs and oddities from all over the world, was almost empty of sightseers. Jenny's glance fell on two Middle Eastern men who were speaking Arabic next to a display of shrunken heads.

"Who, them?" she demanded. Eyeing the headdresses that topped the men's American-style business suits, she giggled, "They look like shepherds in a Christmas play."

"Not them!" Justin whispered with exasperation. He jerked his head across the room. "Him!"

Justin edged away from the glass case. Slipping behind an old player piano, he glanced out of the corner of his eye. Yes, there he was across the room—a stocky, middle-aged man with sandy hair.

Justin took a deep breath, running his fingers through short, carrot-hued curls. Then he peered around the side of the player piano. The sandy-haired man stood with his back to the Parker family. But Justin had felt the man's gaze on them—just as he had earlier that morning at the Firemen's Museum!

"Hey!" A touch on his shoulder whirled him around. He relaxed when he saw his twin.

"Boy, you're as jumpy as if I were that mummy over there!" Thrusting her own head around the side of the player piano, Jenny demanded, "What are you acting so sneaky about? You're not still thinking someone's following us!"

"Shhh! Not so loud," Justin hissed. He dropped his voice to a whisper. "See that guy? It's the second time I've seen him this morning."

Jenny hunched her shoulders, but at least she kept her voice down. "Oh, Justin, do you have to make a mystery out of everything? So a guy's exploring the waterfront just like we are. That doesn't mean he's spying on us."

"Yeah, maybe you're right." Justin grinned. Maybe the guy thought *they* were following him. In any case, it was time he stopped looking for a mystery under every bush—or behind every player piano—and started enjoying this outing.

"Come on." Jenny started down the aisle. "I want to try that slot machine."

They threaded their way past an assortment of polished rocks and a two-headed pig bottled in formaldehyde, stopping in front of an antique slot machine. Jenny dug into her jeans pockets. She held out three quarters and a penny. "You got another quarter?"

Justin dug a quarter out of his own pocket. His sister dropped them into an opening halfway down the machine, then inserted the penny in the slot on top. It disappeared with a whirring sound. A moment later the machine spit out an egg-shaped piece of copper, now stamped with the words *Ye Olde Curiosity Shop*.

"I'll get it!" Both grabbed for the penny and bumped heads—hard! The stamped coin flew across the floor.

"Did you lose this?"

Justin blinked. A square face topped by sandy hair swam into focus. He scrambled to his feet as he recognized the stocky, middle-aged man. He held out his hand. "Yeah, that's ours."

The stocky stranger gave Justin a long, measured look before he dropped the engraved piece of copper into the boy's palm. His narrowed eyes were steel-gray, like the waters of Puget Sound. Justin shifted uneasily under the man's intent gaze. *Am I supposed to know this guy?*

No, he was sure he'd never seen this man before today. Justin closed his fingers on the flattened penny. "Thanks."

"Any time." With a pleasant nod, the sandy-haired man disappeared out the front door of the trading post.

Jenny got to her feet. She rubbed her forehead. "Boy, Justin, you've got a head as hard as a bowling ball!"

"So this is where you two went." Mom and Dad hurried up to the twins.

"Where to now?" Dad demanded as they filed outside.

Jenny skidded to a stop under a brightly painted totem pole, her brown eyes sparking gold with excitement. "Pike Place Market! We haven't been there in a year."

Dad groaned, running long fingers through his rusty, close-cropped hair. "Wouldn't you kids like to see the ships? Pike Place is much too far for an old man to climb."

Justin glanced at his father's lean, freckled face. He *did* look tired.

Ron Parker worked long hours as a computer analyst consultant for Boeing, the airplane manufacturing company in Seattle, Washington. Just the day before, Dad had promised his family that his latest project was nearing an end and that the weekend belonged to them. When Saturday dawned clear and crisp, Justin and Jenny had begged for this trip to the waterfront.

"Come on, Dad! You need some exercise." Jenny poked her father on his flat stomach.

"All right," Dad gave in. "But you'll have to carry me if I don't make it!"

The climb from the waterfront to Pike Place Market involved flight after flight of steep cement steps. Pausing on a landing to catch his breath, Justin glanced back down the long stairway. The steps were empty except for one stocky, sandy-haired man who rested his elbows on the railing below.

He's out of shape too, Justin thought. Then he realized that he himself had fallen well behind the rest of his family. He sprinted to catch up.

Pike Place Market felt hot after the chill sea breeze of the waterfront. The strong smells of freshly caught seafood mingled with the smoke of burning incense and frying chicken gizzards. Justin drew in an appreciative breath. "Mmm. I'm hungry!"

"You're always hungry," Jenny retorted. "Come on."

"Look at the size of that salmon!" Justin licked his lips as a muscular young man tossed a silvery fish from his overflowing cart to the fish vendor behind the nearest counter. "I could eat the whole thing!"

Jenny peeped into a wooden case where a tangle of saltwater crabs snapped their pincers. Grinning, Justin shoved her toward the open box. Jenny let out a squawk and grabbed at the side of the case. Recovering her balance, she elbowed him sharply. "That wasn't funny!"

Mom and Dad caught up before Jenny could take revenge. The four Parkers threaded their way past the seafood to the vegetable and flower stalls.

Justin caught sight of the stocky stranger from Ye Olde Curiosity Shop fingering a leather belt two stalls away. The man cast a sideways glance at the Parkers. Justin frowned. Then, remembering his resolution, he changed the frown to a smile. "Hi, there!" he called with a cheerful wave. "I see you made it up OK."

The sandy-haired man looked startled, but he waved before vanishing again.

Justin was starved by the time they made their way back down to the waterfront. Jenny poked him in the ribs as his stomach growled so loudly that a passing tourist stared. "Mom! Dad! We'd better feed Justin. He's embarrassing me."

Stopping at one of the fast-food stands that lined the waterfront, Dad let them choose their favorites. Even Justin had to agree that the generous helpings of breaded oysters, clams, scallops, and french fries should tide him over until suppertime.

They carried the heaping platters to a picnic area that over-looked the water. Dad asked the blessing on the food, then glanced around the stone table. "Hey, guys, where's the vinegar? We can't eat this without vinegar!"

Justin jumped to his feet. "I'll go get some."

Hurrying back to the seafood stand, Justin picked up the garlic vinegar his father loved on fries and seafood, then started back. He had just reached the picnic area when a sudden glint of light caught the corner of his eye. Skidding to a stop, he stared.

The man with sandy hair sat at the far end of the picnic area. The noon sun reflected off the metallic trim of the binoculars he held tight against his eyes. They were focused in the direction of the Parkers.

Him again! Justin's hazel eyes narrowed. He'd done like Jenny said. He'd tried to stop building a mystery out of every tourist who visited the same attractions as the Parkers. But those binoculars were a little too much for coincidence.

Justin hurried back to his own table. Sliding into his seat, he glanced across the picnic area. The table where the man sat was tucked behind a stone pillar. But now that he knew the stocky stranger was there, he could make out the tips of the binoculars sticking out.

Leaning over to his sister, he hissed, "Psst! Jenny!"

Jenny tossed a french fry to a seagull perched on a nearby bench. The seagull dived, scooping up the treat in midair. "Did you say something?"

Justin jerked his head impatiently. "Check out behind that pillar. It's the guy from the Curiosity Shop! And Pike Place Market."

Jenny stared at the stone pillar. "So what?"

"Don't stare at him!" Justin hissed. "We don't want him to know we know he's there." He lowered his voice. "See those binoculars? They're pointed right at us. I told you he's following us."

"All I see is a guy watching the boats." Jenny waved a hand toward two sailing boats sliding out of their mooring at the end of the wharf. "And my brother making a fool of himself."

"He *is* watching us!" Justin muttered stubbornly, but he didn't bring up the subject again.

The stranger was gone by the time the Parkers had finished eating. Dad stood up and stretched. "Ready to head home, kids?" he suggested hopefully.

"Home?" Jenny's face clouded over. "But you said we could go to Deer Island!"

"Did I say that?" Dad's reddish-brown eyebrows rose high. "You know my memory's been a little hazy lately."

Justin glanced at his watch. "The next ferry leaves in five minutes. We can catch it if we hurry."

"But I'm sure there was some business I had to take care of this afternoon." His eyebrows knit together with concentration.

"Oh, now I remember!" Dad snapped his fingers and grinned. "That business was on Deer Island!"

"You didn't forget, Dad!" Jenny said reproachfully. "Now, stop teasing us! We're going to miss the ferry."

The Parkers reached the ferry dock just as the gangplank was being pulled in. Justin glanced back as he boarded, but if the stranger really had been following them, he was no longer anywhere in sight. Justin and Jenny hurried to the open prow of the ferry, leaving their parents to find seats in the enclosed passenger deck.

An icy sea breeze slapped Justin in the face, carrying with it the familiar tang of salt water. Pulling his jacket tight around his neck, he leaned over the rail. Far off to his left, the green hump of Vashon Island rose above the waters of the Sound. Straight ahead, the outline of the smaller island—now a state park—the Parkers had years earlier nicknamed Deer Island was growing rapidly.

The foghorn blasted as the ferry bumped gently against the massive, wooden piles of the dock. Justin and Jenny hurried to join their parents. Dad stopped at the bottom of the gangplank, one hand shielding his eyes as he scanned the docks.

"He said he'd be here," he muttered.

For the first time, Justin wondered what business his father could have on the island, but Dad had already dropped his hand. He strode rapidly along the boardwalk toward the clustered buildings of the ranger station. "Come on, you guys. You wanted some exercise? So let's see who can beat me around the island!"

Jenny giggled as a sleek yearling deer butted her gently. A herd of deer had been released onto the island years before, the reason for the Parker's nickname. They had multiplied and were now tame enough to be fed by hand.

Mom and Jenny opted to stay and feed the deer. But Dad and Justin wandered down to the shore where a hiking trail had been cut through the brush and evergreen trees that cloaked the island. It took them less than an hour to hike around the shoreline.

Justin scrambled down the bank to the water's edge where he

RACE FOR THE SECRET CODE

had spotted a large pink mollusk shell. Picking it up, he turned to study the shoreline. They were almost back to the landing, and somewhere along in here was a hideout the twins had found years earlier. It had been a long time since the Parkers visited the island, but he was sure the place was somewhere nearby. He had just spotted a familiar Santa-shaped stone when he heard his father exclaim with relief, "There he is!"

Glancing up the bank, Justin's eyes widened at the strange figure moving up the trail from the landing. It was a man with long, white robes and the same flowing headdress the Arab tourists had worn in the Curiosity Shop. Dad hurried to meet him. Grabbing him by the shoulders, the black-bearded stranger kissed him on both cheeks.

Seattle's day for the Middle East! Justin grinned to himself.

Perched on a boulder at the water's edge, he watched as the two men walked slowly back down the trail, heads close together in earnest conversation.

Snap! The breaking twig drew Justin's attention up the bank. He leaned forward with sudden interest. Yes, there it was—a sandy flash among the evergreen branches overhanging the trail!

A man slipped into the shade of a tamarack—a man Justin had already seen too often that day. And this time there could be no mistake about what the stranger was doing. The binoculars in his hands were trained on Dad and his companion.

What does this guy want with my family? Sliding down from the boulder, Justin started angrily up the bank. The man had no right to be following them around all day!

The intruder was too intent on watching the men up the trail to notice the boy circling quietly around behind him. Tapping him on the shoulder, Justin demanded, "Why are you spying on my father? You have no right to—"

But before he had finished speaking, the binoculars dropped. A hard hand clamped over his mouth. A moment later, Justin found himself being dragged helplessly into the tangle of underbrush!

Chapter Two

THE STRANGER

Wind-gnarled branches grabbed at Justin's jacket as the stranger dragged him through the brush. The sharp edges of the binoculars dug painfully into his back, and the hand clamped over his nose and mouth was slowly smothering him. All the warnings his parents had given him about men who preyed on children and teens swept through his mind.

Then he could breathe again! Still holding his hand lightly over Justin's mouth, his captor murmured in his ear, "Will you promise not to scream if I let you go?"

Justin managed a nod. Suddenly, he was free. Wiping the back of his hand across his mouth, he glanced around. He was in a small, grassy clearing closed in by bushes and stunted trees.

The boy looked sideways at his captor, tensing for a dash into the underbrush. But the sandy-haired man made no threatening moves. Instead, he leaned back against the trunk of a tree and crossed his arms. He sighed. "Well, kid! What am I supposed to do with you?"

The man shook his head. "I'll say this much, you have a sharp eye. None of the rest of your family even noticed me."

Justin refused to be sidetracked by the man's compliment.

"Who are you?" he demanded, his anger stiffened by the long rip he'd just discovered in his new winter jacket. "Why were you spying on us? And why did you drag me in here?"

"To keep you quiet!" Unfolding his arms, the stocky stranger straightened up from the tree. "You, boy, have just about managed to spoil an operation that's taken months to set up."

Justin eyed his captor warily. This man didn't sound like a kidnapper. His square face was stern, and his voice had the crisp, authoritative tones of a man used to giving orders. "What operation? Are you a cop?"

The stranger gave Justin the same measured look he had given him in the Curiosity Shop. Shifting uncomfortably, Justin glanced toward the underbrush. Maybe now was the time to make a break for freedom.

But before he could move, the man broke his silence. "You look like an intelligent young man," he said slowly. "And an honest one. I guess you deserve to know what you've stumbled into."

He lifted his broad shoulders in a shrug. "I don't have much choice now, anyway. Not unless I'm prepared to silence you permanently."

Justin drew in a sharp breath.

The sandy-haired man thrust out an arm as he tensed to run. "Hey, kid, I was teasing!" The steel-gray eyes surveyed Justin thoughtfully. "Can I trust you to keep a secret?"

Justin hadn't seen any humor in the man's joke. He scowled, his freckled face hard with suspicion. "What kind of a secret?"

"A secret vital to the security of our country." The stranger's tone was now sharp. "You asked if I'm a cop. I'm not, I'm a government agent. Do you know what that means, kid?"

Justin nodded, his eyes widening with sudden excitement. He'd read enough books and watched enough TV to know about government agents and spy operations. "You mean a secret agent? Like the CIA?"

He studied the stocky stranger with new respect. The man did look sort of like Justin's idea of a secret agent. The thin, straight line of his mouth gave his square features a grim look. Then there were those steel-gray eyes that saw everything.

Glancing up, Justin caught a look of amusement in the gray eyes. He flushed red as he realized how transparent his thoughts had been. Seeing his embarrassment, the stranger's shrewd gaze warmed to a sudden smile. It was a smile that completely transformed the square features, and Justin couldn't help grinning back. For the first time, he found himself relaxing.

"I really am a government agent," the man said gently. Pulling out his wallet, he flipped it open to what looked like a badge. Justin caught the words *National Security Agency* before the man slapped the wallet shut and slipped it back into his pocket.

"Special Agent Grady O'Brian. Just call me Grady. I work for the National Security Agency. You could say we're related to the Central Intelligence Agency. At least we work together on occasion. But the CIA has operations all over the world. We worry only about threats to the security of our own country."

"You mean spies, and terrorists, and all that stuff?" Justin gave an understanding nod, then frowned. "But what does that have to do with us? Why are you following my dad? He's not a spy!"

The sandy-haired man didn't answer, and the thin line of his mouth was grim again. Justin's thoughts flickered back over the events of the day—not just Grady himself, but the Arabs in the

Curiosity Shop and the mysterious appearance of his father's robed companion. A dozen recent news stories of the Middle East flashed through his mind.

"It's the Arabs, isn't it?" he burst out. "I'll bet that's it! They're one of those Muslim terrorist groups. That's why you followed us. You knew my dad was going to meet that Arab!"

"Shhh!" Grady clapped a hand over Justin's mouth as his voice rose with excitement. He threw a cautious glance around the clearing. "Don't say that so loud."

Letting go of Justin, Grady rubbed a hand across his face. "Look, kid, you've really put me in a difficult situation. First, you caught me trailing this man. Now you've figured out our entire operation. If you start talking around, you could ruin any chance we have of closing in on these terrorists. Do you understand what I'm saying?"

Justin understood all right. Everything he'd read had taught him how important complete secrecy was to a government operation. One small leak of information to the bad guys, and the good guys' entire plan would be blown.

"I won't tell anyone," he promised quickly. He hesitated, then added, "Except . . . well, I should tell Mom and Dad."

"No!"

Justin blinked at the explosive order.

"We can't afford the slightest risk of alerting the men we're after," Grady O'Brian said more quietly. "If your mom and dad are like other parents, the first thing they'd do is get on the phone to check out your story. Your dad might even mention it to his Arab friend."

The guy could be right, Justin admitted to himself, but aloud, he protested, "I don't keep secrets from my parents!"

"But this isn't your secret," the sandy-haired man cut in sharply. "It's mine! Are you trying to tell me you've never kept a secret before? I'm sure your friends love it when you blab to your parents everything they tell you in confidence."

"Of course I don't blab my friends' secrets!" Justin answered indignantly.

"So all I'm asking is that you do the same for me—keep a secret that's not yours to tell anyway. You just happened to stumble over something that's none of your business. And you'll be doing your country a big disfavor if you open your mouth about it."

It wasn't quite the same, but Justin saw the government agent's point. He gave a reluctant nod. Grady patted him on the shoulder.

"Thanks, kid. Maybe someday you can impress everyone with today's adventures. But right now you just go on back to your family and forget this ever happened."

Justin had no wish to hang around. He was already pushing into the underbrush when Grady O'Brian's call stopped him.

"Don't forget, kid!" There was no longer a smile in the steel-gray eyes. "Your country is counting on you to keep quiet. If this operation leaks out, we'll know who's responsible."

Chapter Three

A RELUCTANT RIDE

Neither Dad nor his Arab companion were in sight when Justin got back to the trail. He trotted down the path. Now that he had left the government agent behind, the whole adventure seemed a little unreal. But what a story it would have made to tell his friends!

He hadn't gone far when he saw Jenny hurrying up the trail to meet him. "Justin, where have you been? Dad's been looking all over for you." Her brown eyes narrowed as she saw his torn jacket and scuffed jeans. "What happened to you?"

"Sorry, I can't tell you." Justin's chest swelled with importance. He lowered his voice to a mysterious whisper. "It's a matter of national security!"

"Right!" Jenny scoffed. She broke into a run. "Come on. We're going to miss the ferry."

When they arrived at the ferry dock, Mom and Dad were talking with a tall young man in a park ranger's uniform. "No, I'm alone here right now," the ranger said. "My boss and his wife are off to Hawaii for a month. Of course, there aren't many visitors in the winter."

Mom's eyebrows rose high as she caught sight of Justin. "There you are! Where did you disappear . . . oh, Justin, your jacket! What happened?"

The mournful bellow of the incoming ferry cut her off, to Justin's relief. They had crossed Puget Sound again and were driving home when Jenny leaned over the front seat of the car. "Hey, Dad, who was that Arab guy you were talking to?"

"Who, Abdul?" Dad glanced into the rearview mirror. "Just a contact from work. He wanted to see me before leaving the country tonight."

"Deer Island sure seems like a funny place for a business meeting."

"That's your fault." Dad grinned back at his daughter. "I told Abdul I'd already promised my family a day on the waterfront, so we agreed to meet on Deer Island."

Dad turned off the freeway into their own neighborhood. "Abdul el Kutub is an interesting man. I'll have to introduce you kids to him on his next trip. He's done a lot to improve Arab relations with the U.S."

That's what you think! Justin thought. Maybe someday he'd get a chance to tell his father about the mysterious Arab. By that time Abdul el Kutub would probably be under arrest for international terrorism.

Justin sat up straight as a sudden thought occurred to him. Did Grady O'Brian know that this Abdul was flying out of the country tonight? It would be awful if the terrorist escaped. If there was only some way to let the government agent know!

Catching a curious glance from his sister, Justin forced himself to relax against the seat. After all, the government had been tracking terrorists for a long time without his help. Besides, the sandy-haired agent had told Justin to forget the whole thing, and that's what he'd better do.

Tuesday evening, the whole family drove to Sea-Tac Airport to see off their best friend, Danny Nguyen, and his grandfather. Only a few weeks earlier, they had helped Danny and his grandfather bring about the arrest of the dreaded Dragon Tong that had been terrorizing the Vietnamese community. While the insurance company rebuilt the destroyed La Vie Restaurant, Mr. Nguyen was taking Danny on a long-dreamed-of trip to his birthplace in Vietnam.

Justin waved as Danny disappeared through the security checkpoint. *Now who am I going to hang out with?*

By Friday, Justin had nearly forgotten Grady O'Brian and the incident on Deer Island. School was out that day, so Dad had arranged for the twins to tour the prototype of Boeing's newest airbus. Jenny, who had zero interest in engineering, had opted out. But Justin dreamed of designing planes even bigger and better than his father's someday, and he eagerly poked his nose into every corner of the assembly plant that the security guards would allow him.

It was almost noon when the engineer who had been his tour guide dropped him off in front of the research facility where his father worked. Waving his thanks, Justin pulled out the security pass his father had given him and started toward the gate that led into the research complex. But he had taken only a few steps when he stopped short.

The security guard, whose job it was to check everyone who went in and out of the research facility, was sitting in a guard box beside the gate. In front of the guard box, handing up a plastic card through the open window, was a stocky figure Justin had never expected to see again.

The government agent turned around, his gray eyes narrowing as he spotted Justin. Snatching his card from the security guard's hand, Grady started toward Justin with long, rapid strides.

"What are you doing here, Gr—" Steel-strong fingers dug into Justin's upper arm, cutting off his exclamation.

"Be quiet, boy!" Grady hissed in Justin's ear.

"Hey, Justin!" The security guard leaned out of the window of the guard box. "Are you okay?"

Grady loosened his grip on Justin's arm, but he gave a warning shake of his head. Justin waved his free hand at the security guard. "Yeah, I'm fine! He's a friend."

But as Grady hurried him down the sidewalk, Justin demanded again, "What *are* you doing here? I thought you were supposed to be tailing that Arab guy."

Grady didn't answer. He stopped beside a dark blue sedan parked just outside the front gate. Justin pulled hard against the man's steel grip. "Hey, I'm not going anywhere with you! I'm supposed to be meeting my dad."

Opening the passenger door, Grady gave Justin a gentle shove. "We're just going to have a little talk! Then I'll bring you back."

Without kicking and screaming and making a general idiot of himself, Justin didn't see any choice. Reluctantly, he climbed into the car. Slamming the door behind him, Grady hurried around to the driver's side. The agent's hand went to the door as the car pulled away from the curb, and Justin heard a sharp click. He was locked in!

Justin was now both angry and scared. Was this man really a government agent as he'd said? And where was he taking him? Would he really bring him back? Justin glanced sideways. Grady whistled softly under his breath, his face thoughtful as he maneuvered in and out of traffic. But he offered no explanation.

Turning his back, Justin stared defiantly out the window. He made careful mental notes of each change of direction. If this man didn't keep his promise, he'd find his own way back.

After a few minutes Grady turned onto a wide street lined with tall, dingy apartment buildings. Pulling into an alley, Justin heard a click as the doors were unlocked. But Grady made no move to get out of the car. Instead, he turned to Justin.

"Look, kid, I'm sorry," he said. "I had to get you out of there before that guard started asking questions."

"But, why?" A bewildered interest was beginning to replace Justin's anger. "I don't underst—"

"You'll get an explanation soon enough!" Grady cut in. He jerked his head toward the apartment building on the left. "Let's go."

Taking hold of Justin's arm again, Grady guided him toward a side door in the apartment building, but this time his grip was loose. Inside, he pushed Justin ahead of him up a wooden staircase. When they had climbed two flights, he turned into a narrow, dimly lit hallway. Stopping in front of the last door on the right, he gave two rapid taps.

Grady didn't wait for an answer. Slipping a key into the lock, he pushed the door open. Justin, still unsure, stopped stubbornly in the doorway. He glanced around. The apartment was small and shabby with furniture that looked like rejects from a second-hand store. At the far end of the combination living room/kitchen, a door stood open leading into a tiny bedroom.

Across the room, a man hunched over a computer keyboard. Justin eyed the computer with admiration. He knew plenty about computers, and this had to be one of the most expensive and sophisticated Justin had ever seen.

Grady pushed Justin into the room. "Hacker, we've got a problem!" he said abruptly.

The man at the computer spun around in his chair. He was in his twenties with pale eyes and long, unwashed blonde hair tied in a ponytail. He gave Justin a long, unfriendly look. "What's the kid doing here?"

Giving Justin a gentle shove toward the sofa, Grady crossed the room to the computer desk.

Justin watched while Grady spoke in low, urgent tones. The younger man's sharp features grew sullen. Shaking his head angrily, he let out a violent curse.

"It isn't as bad as that." Grady's low voice was firm. "I think the boy could be helpful."

The two men glanced up suddenly. Catching Justin's interested gaze, Grady strode over to the front door and locked it. "It isn't that I don't trust you," he told Justin, dropping the key into his pocket. "But we really do need to have that talk. You just stay put, and we'll be back in a moment."

Grady gave a jerk of the head. With obvious reluctance, Hacker got to his feet and followed him into the bedroom. Ignoring Grady's order, Justin sprang to his feet as soon as the door closed behind the two men. He was trying the front door when the two men returned. Grady's thin lips twitched as Justin dropped his hand guiltily from the locked knob, but he only motioned the boy back to the sofa.

Obeying, Justin glanced across the room. The ponytailed Hacker was already bent over the computer keyboard again. A computer hacker, he knew, was someone who was an expert at accessing computers. This man certainly deserved his nickname! His long, thin fingers flew across the keys.

Dropping into a nearby armchair, Grady gave Justin a thoughtful look. But Justin had had enough of waiting. Scooting forward to the edge of the sofa, he burst out belligerently, "So! Are you going to tell me why you're still following my dad around? If you really *were* a government agent, you'd know that Abdul el Kutub guy left the country a long time ago."

"What did you say?" Grady leaned forward, his steel-gray eyes suddenly alert.

"I said that Abdul el Kutub guy already left the country." Justin was puzzled by the sharpness of Grady's tone.

Grady relaxed back into his seat. "Of course, I know. I hadn't realized you were personally acquainted with the man," he said mildly.

"Oh, I'm not!" Justin assured him. "It was my dad who told me he was leaving the country."

"Yes, we know that. Unfortunately, he'll be back." The sandy-haired man broke off. After a moment's silence, he said slowly, "Justin, I'd hoped never to see you again. Unfortunately, you decided to visit your father's office on the same day I chose to check out that facility. But maybe we can use this situation to both our advantages."

"You know my name?" Justin demanded, surprised.

"It's my job to know things. You'd be surprised at all I know about you and your family." Grady smiled. Justin felt his suspicions ebbing, and he couldn't help grinning back. Uncertainly he said, "Then . . . you really *are* a government agent."

"Of course!" Grady said, still smiling. "But you're right to be cautious. I wish I could bring someone in to verify who I am, but that would jeopardize the security of this mission."

Taking out his wallet, Grady again flipped it open to the badge that read *National Security Agency* and handed it to Justin. He studied it closely. It sure looked authentic.

Handing back the wallet, he eyed the government agent.

There was something solid and completely trustworthy about the stocky figure and authoritative voice. Justin's tension ebbed away. He relaxed. "Yeah, I believe you."

"Thank you." Grady slid his wallet back into his pocket, then clasped his muscular fingers around one knee. "Justin, I'm going to do something right now that I've never done before. I'm going to have to give you classified information. I'll expect you to keep this information strictly in confidence."

Justin perked up his ears. At last, he was going to find out what this was all about!

"For some time, certain highly classified military projects developed by Boeing have been falling into the hands of several very dangerous Middle East factions," Grady explained. "We finally traced the leak to Abdul el Kutub's regular visits to Seattle."

"You mean, Abdul's been stealing government secrets and

selling them to the Middle East?" Justin sat up straight. Then he frowned. "But . . . if you know it's Abdul, why don't you just arrest him? And what were you doing at my dad's research facility? . . . Of course!" He snapped his fingers. "You want to know who's giving him the information. It's got to be someone in the research department."

Grady nodded approval. "That's right. Someone inside Boeing has been feeding information to Abdul. And now Abdul is offering the plans of a new classified military project to the highest Middle Eastern bidder—a project so new it hasn't even been finished."

"What kind of a project?" Justin's unease was giving way to interest. This was better than a movie!

Grady was silent for a moment. Then he said, "Do you know what a radar detection system is, Justin?"

Justin nodded. He'd read about radar often enough in science magazines. Radar systems used radio waves to detect objects too far away to be seen.

"Then you know that modern armies have depended largely on radar for locating and identifying hostile ships, planes, and missiles. That makes radar invisibility a big advantage in a war."

"You mean, like the F-117A Stealth Fighter," Justin interrupted with excitement.

"Right!" Grady said with another approving nod. "Unfortunately, radar invisibility isn't enough anymore."

The scrape of a chair made Justin glance across the room. The ponytailed Hacker had swiveled away from his computer and was listening to Grady's explanation. His sharp features showed no expression, but Justin had the uneasy feeling that there was amusement behind his pale eyes. Turning back to Grady, Justin demanded, "So what does this have to do with my dad?"

"Everything! For years, your father's been working on a project they call an 'invisibility shield'—a screen that works equally well against radar detectors and long-range surveillance cameras. They weren't having much success until a recent breakthrough. Now the GP145—your father's project—is finally nearing completion."

The stocky agent leaned forward. "Think what that means, Justin! Military installations, aircraft, ships, even missiles, completely invisible to enemy detection."

"Wow!" Justin grinned back, then added doubtfully, "So . . . is this project of my dad's the one Abdul is trying to sell?"

Grady's grin vanished. "Unfortunately, yes. If Abdul sold the GP145 to some terrorist group or a country hostile to the U.S.— well, I'm sure you're smart enough to figure it out. Nothing we have could detect a missile equipped with that invisibility shield!"

Almost in a whisper, Justin answered, "They could blow up any part of the world they wanted!"

"You see why we can't just arrest Abdul." Grady's mouth was grim. "We *must* find out who at Boeing is leaking this classified data before it's too late! Before our traitor hands the invisibility shield over to Abdul el Kutub—or someone else!"

"But why are you telling *me* all this?" Justin demanded, bewildered.

"Because I need your help," Grady answered soberly. "You've certainly proved that you can be trusted."

As Justin flushed with embarrassment and pleasure, he went on, "I was at Boeing this afternoon to get vital information. I ran the risk of alerting the traitor to our investigation. But if you can get the information we need—information to which your father has access—then no one at Boeing will know they are being investigated until it is too late."

"You mean, you just want me to ask my dad to get you some information?" Justin said with relief. "Sure, I can do that! My dad would be glad to help."

"No!"

Justin looked at Grady in surprise.

The agent shook his head. "No one in Boeing—certainly not your father—must know of this investigation! You'll have to get that information without telling him, or anyone else, what you've seen or heard here today."

"Now wait a minute!" Justin sat bolt upright, his freckled face indignant. "You asked me to keep your secret, and I did. But this is different. There's no way I'm going to spy on my own dad. I'm sorry, but you're just going to have to find someone else to get your information."

"I'm afraid you don't understand, Justin." Grady's square features were suddenly stern. "This isn't a request—it's an order! And you will *not* say anything to your father or anyone else. Because if you don't cooperate, your father will immediately find himself under arrest for international espionage!"

Chapter Four

SPY GAMES

Justin couldn't believe his ears! He jumped angrily to his feet. "What do you mean, you'll arrest my dad? Are you trying to say he's the spy?"

The steel-gray eyes were still cold. "Your father is one of the few people who has complete access to the plans and computer data. And you yourself saw him passing classified information to Abdul."

Justin had a sudden horrifying mental picture of his father and Abdul el Kutub in earnest conversation on a lonely back trail of Deer Island. He pushed away the thought. Whatever the purpose of his father's meeting with Abdul, it had nothing to do with this.

"I don't believe it. I didn't see my dad pass anything to Abdul." Justin started toward the door, his jaw thrust out with angry determination.

"I thought you would put the welfare of your country ahead of your own feelings," Grady said sternly. "Your family will be in danger too if the GP145 falls into the wrong hands."

Justin dropped his hand from the doorknob. "But I *know* my dad! He'd never *think* of selling government secrets."

"Justin, I believe you." The kindness in Grady's voice startled Justin. *He's just doing his job,* he realized with astonishment. *He'd really like to help me!*

"I admit I didn't tell you everything the other day," Grady went on gently. "Yes, we've been following Abdul, but we've been following your father as well. His contacts with Abdul made him a suspect."

Grady pressed the tips of his fingers together, his square features thoughtful. "No, I'm convinced now your father isn't the one we want. I think someone else is using him to hand the computer CDs over to Abdul. I'm sure your dad thinks he's passing along unclassified information."

"Well, I didn't see my dad passing any computer CDs," Justin said stubbornly. "And if you think he's innocent, why did you say you'd arrest . . ."

Grady cut him off with a sharp gesture. "The fact is that your father is the only one with access to the GP145 who has had *any* contact with Abdul. My superiors believe that your father is the traitor. They wanted me to pull him in when we caught him with Abdul last Saturday. But I convinced them that we needed more evidence."

With stern authority he added, "You have no choice but to cooperate with me. The only way to get your father off the hook is to catch the real traitor. If we don't, your father will always be under suspicion of espionage. And if my superiors think they have enough evidence, they'll arrest him and send him to jail. By that time, the real traitor will have sold that invisibility shield to the highest bidder."

"Then you've *got* to let me talk to my dad!" Justin jumped to his feet again. "If someone's really passing him those CDs, I'm sure he can explain. You've *got* to let him prove he's innocent!"

"Justin, your father isn't the only one at stake here," Grady said grimly. "The entire security of our country rests on our unmasking that spy. If the real traitor suspects that your father knows the truth about what's going on, he'll disappear. Ron Parker will have his chance to prove his innocence, but not until we've caught the real traitor."

Justin wasn't completely convinced, but he nodded a reluctant agreement. "So what do you want me to do?"

"You can help by getting the information we need. First, we need to know if your father could reproduce that invisibility shield himself if necessary. Then, we need to know exactly when the project will be finished. That's when Abdul and his accomplice will make their move. And we need to be waiting for them."

"That shouldn't be too hard to find out," Justin admitted. He glanced back across the room. Hacker was hunched over the computer again. "Do you want me to call when I get the information?"

"Not directly, but you can use my beeper." Grady pulled out the small notebook he carried. Tearing out a sheet of paper, he scribbled numbers on it. "Here's my number. Page me when you've got the information, and I'll call back as soon as I can. Just don't show it to anyone. And don't use it unless you have to."

Grady dropped Justin off a block short of the Boeing research facility. As he got out of the car, the agent reached over and patted him on the shoulder. "Don't look so gloomy, kid. We'll nail these guys."

Grady's cheerful self-confidence didn't make Justin feel much better. After all, it wasn't *his* father who was being accused of international espionage. Glancing at his watch, Justin broke into a run.

But Dad was still in a meeting when he arrived out of breath at his father's third-floor office. Justin did his best to act natural when the meeting was over. But it wasn't easy, and as they drove home, he stared silently out the window.

"What's the matter, son?" Dad raised an eyebrow at Justin's preoccupied frown. "Didn't you like the tour?"

Justin had totally forgotten about the new Boeing airbus. Sitting up straight, he forced a smile. "Sure, Dad! It was great. Thanks."

He paused, then added, "You look awfully tired, Dad. I guess that project's really getting you down."

Dad ran a weary hand over his face. "Yes, I *am* tired. I'll be glad when the whole thing is done."

"But *when* will it be done?"

As soon as the words left his mouth, Justin knew he had spoken too urgently. Giving him a sharp look, Dad said, "I know I haven't had much time for you kids lately. Just hang in there a few more days."

So it'll be finished in just a few more days! Keeping his voice casual, Justin said, "I guess you're really important at Boeing, aren't you, Dad? I mean, for you to be in charge of an important project like that."

Dad showed no suspicion of Justin's questions. "Where did you get the idea I was in charge of this project?" he asked now, glancing curiously across at Justin.

"You mean . . . you're not?" Justin sat up straight in aston-ishment. "But I thought it was your project."

"I'll take that as a compliment, son," Dad said with a chuckle. "No, I just head up the computer side of the project. The scientists and engineers are the ones who come up with the ideas and technical data for these projects."

"So you couldn't build one of your projects out of your head?" Justin tried not to sound too anxious. "Even after working on it all those months?"

Dad shook his head. "I don't think even a scientist could do that. There's just too much data involved. The scientists only know the part of the project they're working on. It takes the computers to put it all together." A sudden grin relaxed the tired lines of his mouth. "*And* computer analysts like me."

Satisfied, Justin leaned back in his seat. This had been easier than he'd expected. But then, he thought with a twinge of guilt, Dad had no reason to hide anything from his son. Justin dismissed the thought firmly. After all, he was only doing this to help his father.

He punched in Grady's beeper number as soon as he got home. But though he lay awake until midnight, the government agent didn't call. Nor did he call the next day—or the next. Justin, who normally hated answering the phone, found himself jumping to his feet every time it rang.

"Expecting a girl to call?" Jenny teased.

Justin only grinned at her, but as two more days went by, he grew restless and irritable. Dad was now working until midnight or later every night, and on two nights he didn't come home at all.

On Wednesday Justin flunked the first test of his school

career—a science test, at that! But he barely glanced at the grade before stuffing it into his backpack. Why hadn't Grady called if he needed that information so urgently?

That very evening Grady finally called. "It's for you, Justin," Mom announced. "Some man."

"I'll take it in the office," Justin said. Catching his sister's curious glance, he added quickly, "It's probably my science teacher. You know, that test I flunked."

Justin dashed downstairs to his mother's basement office. Locking the door behind him, he grabbed the phone and said, "I've been trying to reach you for days!"

Grady's crisp tones were hurried and tired. "Is it finished?"

Justin shook his head. "No, I don't think so, but it could be any day. Dad didn't even come home last night. That's always a sign they're almost finished."

"I've got to have that information as soon as possible!" Grady said sharply. "Every hour counts."

Justin only said, "I'll call when I find out. And about my dad . . ."

He repeated all his father had told him about the project. "So my dad doesn't know how to build that invisibility shield," he finished eagerly. "That proves he's innocent, doesn't it?"

There was a silence on the other end of the line. Grady's voice sounded strange when he finally spoke. "Justin, your father is listed as one of the few men with access to the entire project. Are you telling me he's only a computer hacker?"

Justin found himself repeating his father's words. "The scientists couldn't build the thing without the computer analysts to put all their data together."

"So the computer's the only one who knows everything about the project." Grady sounded far away as though he were talking to himself or someone else in the room. Then his voice warmed with approval. "Thanks, Justin! You've done your country a great service."

Hanging up the phone, Justin unlocked the office door. Jenny was waiting right outside. "Since when is your science teacher a man?" she demanded. "And why did you lock the office door?"

The sound of the front door opening saved him from answering.

Justin followed Jenny upstairs. By the time they reached the living room, Dad had already dropped his briefcase onto a chair and was pulling off his tie. His eyes were rimmed with red, and he rubbed a weary hand over two days of beard stubble. "What a marathon! But we all voted to push on until we had finished."

Justin drew in a sharp breath. Jenny asked eagerly, "You mean the project's finished? Can you tell us now what you were working on? Is it still a secret?"

"Yes, Jenny it's finished. Right down to the very last data entry."

Justin edged toward the hall. If only Grady had called just half an hour later! As he hurried downstairs, he heard his father say, "No, Jenny, I'm afraid the project's still classified."

Justin lay awake far into the night. He'd punched in Grady's beeper number, but the government agent didn't call back.

Grady still hadn't called by the time they headed for the bus stop the next morning. He had to do something soon! If he waited for Grady to call, it might be too late to save his dad's project.

Jenny gave her brother a sharp jab as he stopped right in the middle of the sidewalk. Planting herself in front of him, she demanded, "What's with you, Justin? You're acting like a zombie!"

When she repeated her question, he shrugged. "I didn't get much sleep last night."

Jenny looked skeptical. "Or maybe it's that science teacher that called? Come on, tell me! Who was it, really?"

Justin didn't answer. Stretching his long legs into a run, he called over his shoulder, "We'd better hurry or we'll miss the bus!"

The bus was nowhere in sight when they reached the corner. Jenny gave her brother a funny look, but Justin ignored her, pulling out his science book and pretending to study. He had made up his mind. Grady had to have that information even if he had to deliver it in person.

On the bus, Jenny was uncharacteristically quiet. Justin knew his twin too well to hope she had forgotten the phone call, but at least she wasn't asking any more awkward questions.

When they got to school, Justin checked his schedule. He had a study hall right before lunch, and the monitor never noticed if anyone sneaked out. He should be able to find Grady's apartment and still be back for science.

Justin shifted restlessly through English class and was out the door before the bell finished ringing. His plan couldn't have gone smoother. A city bus pulled up just as he reached the bus stop. It dropped him in the low-income neighborhood where Grady had taken him the week before. A cold drizzle had started, but not even the slow rain that trickled down the neck of his jacket dampened his growing excitement. He *had*, after all, completed the mission Grady had given him. And wasn't this the sort of adventure every boy dreamed of—working with a real secret agent? As for his father, Grady had promised everything would be all right.

Grady's sure going to be pleased to see me! Justin thought as he trotted down an alley head down, shoulders hunched against the cold. He had mentally saved the country from terrorists and was just receiving a medal from the president when he ran smack into something very solid.

"Ouch!" Stumbling backwards, Justin put out a hand to keep from falling. A vague impression of something dark and square crystallized into the rear end of a shiny-new, brown van. He raised his hand gingerly to his forehead. It came away sticky. *Blood!* he thought, but the stain on his fingers was fluorescent orange.

Blinking the drizzle from his eyelashes, Justin saw streaks of wet paint splashed in a tic-tac-toe pattern across the back of the van. Behind the van, fresh graffiti blazed in the same fluorescent orange across a brick wall. Justin grinned as he stooped to wipe his fingers on a tuft of grass. After today, the van's owner would know better than to leave a new and expensive vehicle unwatched in this section of town.

He stopped grinning as he glanced at his watch. It was later than he thought—almost noon. He'd have to hurry if he was going to make it back to school before he was missed.

He broke into a run. In the drizzle and mist, the shabby brick buildings all looked the same. Then he caught sight of a dark blue sedan in front of an apartment complex. That had to be Grady's car.

He hurried down the street until he reached the blue sedan.

It *was* Grady's! Turning into the alley he tried the side door they had used before. It was unlocked. Slipping inside, he shook the rain from his hair and coat, then bounded up the stairs. Justin turned right and trotted down the hall until he came to the last door. He'd raised his hand to knock when he saw that the door stood open an inch.

He was about to push on it when he caught his father's name. His hand froze on the knob.

"I told you Ron Parker's no scientist!" It was Grady. "What good would it do for those goons to grab him? He's got the data stored in that computer, but it isn't in his brain!"

Justin inched the door open a little wider. Now he could see Grady standing over the computer desk, his square face tight with annoyance. Hacker glared up at the stocky agent. Neither man seemed to notice the wide-eyed boy standing frozen in the doorway.

Hacker mumbled something. "Absolutely not!" Grady interrupted violently. Picking up the phone, he slammed it down closer to Hacker. "Get on the phone right now! If any of those goons touch Ron Parker, they'll answer to me. And next time check your sources better."

Justin had heard enough. Pushing the door all the way open, he took a step into the room. "What's going on, Grady?" he demanded, his voice unnaturally high. "Who's trying to kidnap my dad?"

Chapter Five

INVISIBILITY SHIELD

Grady whirled around. Justin shrank back at the anger in the gray eyes. His heart skipped a beat as his eyes dropped to the gun in the government agent's right hand. For one long, frozen moment, the boy and the man stared at each other. Then Grady lowered the gun.

"Justin, you scared the wits out of me!" he said. "I thought you were . . ." He slipped the gun back into a holster under his jacket. "Never mind. How'd you get in here, anyway?"

"The . . . the door was open." Justin could have kicked himself. He should have known better than to sneak up on a secret agent. "I didn't mean to startle you."

Grady strode across the room to lock the door. "Hacker, I told you to keep that door locked! One of these days . . ."

"Grady, is someone after you?" Edging farther into the room, Justin went back to his earlier question. "And who are the 'goons' you were talking about? Who's trying to kidnap my dad?"

"Someone's always after me," the sandy-haired agent said, but he stopped to give Justin a pat on the shoulder. "Don't worry about your father."

"But I heard . . . you said someone was trying to grab him!"

"Someone *was* trying to grab your dad," Grady admitted. "That's why we're a little edgy. You see, I wasn't the only one who thought your father knew more than he does. Our enemies planned to kidnap your father and force him to build the invisibility shield for them."

"But I thought the traitor was inside Boeing!" Justin shook his head, confused. "Everybody there knows my dad's not a scientist. And so does Abdul. Why would they try to kidnap him?"

Grady was silent for a moment, then went on, "Since you overheard us, I'll explain. Abdul wasn't trying to grab your father. But since we talked last, I've confirmed that Abdul has offered the GP145 for sale to an Islamic terrorist group. They decided to save the sales price by kidnapping your father and forcing him to build the invisibility shield for them."

Justin frowned. This was getting more and more complicated. Grady gestured toward Hacker, who was speaking in low, angry tones into the telephone.

"Don't worry. My men will keep an eye on your father. And Hacker's making sure they know Ron Parker's only a computer analyst. A most important one, of course." Grady grinned at Justin. "But he'll be safe once they realize he's no scientist."

That made sense. As Justin gave a relieved nod, Grady looked at him sharply. "Now, what are you doing here? And how'd you find this place?"

"You never answered your beeper. And I *had* to talk to you." Justin's voice faltered. "Did I ruin the operation?"

"No, you didn't ruin the operation, but you shouldn't have come here," Grady said. "I guess it was my fault. . . . I left my beeper home last night."

A smile warmed the gray eyes. "To tell the truth, it never occurred to me you'd find your way back. You're quite a kid, Justin! Maybe we'll make an agent out of *you* someday."

Justin swelled with pride. "I didn't think you'd mind when you heard the news," he said eagerly. "Dad came home last night. He says they're done, right down to the last data entry. You said you wanted—"

But Grady was already striding across the room. Grabbing the phone from Hacker, he cut off the younger man's call and began punching out numbers. Justin got to his feet. "Is there anything else you want me to find out?"

Grady glanced up, his hand across the receiver. He flashed Justin a brief smile. "I don't think so. I'll let you know if we need your help again."

"You *will* let me know when they find out that my father's innocent, won't you?" Justin was reluctant to leave, but Grady was already speaking into the phone in low, urgent tones.

"Well . . . I've got to go, or I'll miss my class," Justin said in a louder voice.

Without looking up, Grady tossed him a key. Justin unlocked the door, then glanced back. The sandy-haired agent was nodding as he scribbled across a pad of scratch paper. Placing the key on a low table, Justin went out and shut the door.

Well, that's that! Justin glanced at his watch as he clattered back down the stairs. He'd have to hurry if he was to make it before his science teacher called the attendance roll. Justin broke into a run.

He didn't make it. The drizzle had given way to a heavy rain. Head hunched under his jacket, Justin missed a street sign and had to waste precious time retracing his way to the bus stop. When he finally arrived, a bus was just pulling away, and he had to wait another half hour for the next. This one didn't follow the same route as the earlier bus that had brought him here, and he had to take a second bus to get back to school.

The final bell was already ringing by the time he raced up the front steps of the school. He'd hoped to reach his locker without anyone noticing his entrance, but Jenny was waiting for him just inside the glass doors. She stayed right at his elbow as he walked to his locker.

"Where were you?" she hissed. "You never came to lunch."

Grabbing his backpack from his locker, Justin pushed his way back to the front entrance. Jenny caught up with him as he reached the bottom of the steps. Blocking his way, she demanded, "Justin, answer me! I covered for you as best I could, but you'd better have a good excuse for cutting classes."

Justin groaned inwardly. He'd never been able to fool his sister. But he just couldn't let her know where he had really been.

"It was this awful stomachache," he improvised, trying to look pale as he put one hand to his stomach. "I couldn't eat lunch. It was so bad I had to go to the drugstore and get some antacid."

"Yeah! So why didn't you just ask the school nurse?" Jenny put her hands on her hips. "Come on, Justin! What's going on?"

Justin didn't answer. Jenny gave him a look that said she didn't believe a word of his story. Turning her back on him, she hurried on ahead to scramble aboard the bus. She already had her nose buried in a library book by the time he dropped into the seat beside her, and she kept it there all the way home.

Justin glanced miserably at his sister. As twins, he and Jenny had always been closer than most brothers and sisters. He'd never kept a secret from her—or lied to her.

Well, it wasn't his fault! Justin stared defiantly out the bus window. He'd promised not to tell anyone. And that included Jenny!

Dad had been sleeping when they'd left for school that morning. But he was awake by the time they dropped their backpacks on the kitchen counter. Already, he was looking less exhausted, and supper was a leisurely celebration with Mom bringing out Dad's favorite Chinese dishes. Jenny carefully avoided addressing any remarks to Justin, but she made no mention of his cutting classes.

After supper, Justin stretched out on the living room carpet with the latest *Popular Science*. He leafed through an article on the Armed Forces' latest radar detection systems. That reminded him of what Grady had told him about the invisibility shield. He glanced across the room. Dad and Jenny were bent over a chessboard on the coffee table. Dad's eyes twinkled as he knocked over Jenny's white castle and replaced it with a black knight.

Justin eyed his father curiously. Would he look so relaxed if he were really responsible for a government project so dangerous it could threaten the security of the United States? What would he say if he knew what Justin had done that day?

For the first time, Justin began to wonder if Grady was right about his father. The government agent's information had been wrong once before. Maybe Grady had mixed him up with another man, a real scientist!

Suddenly he *had* to know. After all, Dad was used to his son asking questions about anything remotely scientific. Rolling over on his side, he propped himself up on his elbows. "Uh, Dad? Could you make a plane or . . . or a military base or something invisible? So it couldn't be detected by radar or . . . or cameras."

"Checkmate in one move, Dad!" Knocking her father's knight clear off the chessboard, Jenny rubbed her hands gleefully together.

Dad studied the chessboard with a deep frown. "That's a problem the U.S. military has been working on a long time, Justin," he said absently. "They've tried a lot of things. Hiding missile sites or military bases underground. Camouflaging with dirt and plants. But satellite cameras can usually still pick them out."

Dad reached a long arm across the chessboard. "The military does have a few fighter jets designed to fool radar. They're built with such odd angles that they fool the detection systems into reading them as a bird or some other natural phenomena."

Moving a black pawn out of the way of his castle, he added, "Those old *Popular Science* downstairs have some good articles on camouflage and radar detection. I'll help you find them just as soon as I checkmate your sister here."

"What?" Jenny shrieked. As her face clouded over with dismay, Dad toppled the white king with a flick of a long forefinger.

"I was sure I had you this time!" Jenny wailed.

"Dad, I've already read those articles," Justin interrupted impatiently. "I'm not talking about camouflage or building a plane with weird angles. I'm talking about a shield you could put on a plane or a boat so nothing could detect it."

He held his breath. For a moment, he didn't think his father was going to answer.

"There is no such system presently operable," Dad said slowly. "But it's theoretically possible."

Justin sat up, his freckled face eager. "So how would you go about it? Theoretically, I mean."

Dad laced his fingers behind his head. "A radar detector works with radio waves. The radio waves sent out by the radar system bounce off anything in front of them, say—like incoming planes or missiles. The waves that bounce back tell the radar controller the size and shape of the target and even how far away it is. Of course, that's a pretty simplified explanation."

"So how could you make a plane or missile invisible?" Justin looked doubtful. "I mean, even if you disguised it, all those waves bouncing back would show *something* was out there."

"That's been the problem up until now," Dad agreed. "But there *are* a few things you could try. Theoretically, of course. Only solid, hard objects, like a missile or a plane reflect radar waves. If you could somehow find a way to absorb those radio waves—keep them from bouncing back—your plane or missile wouldn't register on the radar screen. You'd have radar invisibility.

"Of course, you'd still have the problem of satellite TV cameras and surveillance planes. But there's another idea you could try. Long-range surveillance cameras 'see' by interpreting the light waves that bounce back at them. Every object has its own 'light signature.'"

Dad's freckled face lit up with enthusiasm. "Imagine, Justin, if you could create a method—say a shield like you mentioned—that absorbed light and radio waves instead of bouncing them back. At the same time, this shield would project, not the true 'light signature' of the object it protected, but a different one."

"A mirage, you mean!" Justin's eyes widened with excitement. "Like when you see a lake or something out in the desert, and it isn't really there. Boy, if you could do that, you really *would* be invisible. The cameras and radar wouldn't know anything was there at all."

Getting to his feet, Dad stretched his arms over his head. "But to come up with such a 'shield' is a vastly complicated undertaking. So far, it's been a lot easier just to cover a base with dirt or build a fighter that looks like a bird."

Dad glanced down at Jenny who was still brooding over the chessboard. Reaching down, he tipped the pieces off onto the coffee table. "Stop sulking, Jenny! Let's go see if a chocolate-mint sundae won't distract you from your latest defeat."

Justin was quiet for a moment. But as Dad and Jenny started toward the kitchen, he said hesitantly, "Dad, you . . . you aren't working on anything like that, are you?"

There was an awful silence. Puzzled, Justin raised his eyes. His father was standing curiously still in the kitchen doorway. Then he turned slowly around.

"Where did you get that information, Justin?" The question was soft, but very distinct. Justin had never dreamed his easygoing father could sound so cold.

Chapter Six

ABDUL EL KUTUB

"Where did you get that information, Justin?" Dad repeated sternly.

Jenny stared with baffled interest from one freckled face to the other. Justin scrambled to his feet. Dad crossed the living room with long, quick strides.

Gripping Justin hard by the shoulder, he said, "Son, I *must* know what gave you the idea that I was working on this invisibility shield. Think! I know I've never mentioned anything on the subject."

"I . . . I must have overheard it somewhere." Justin's eyes dropped away from his father's hard gaze. His heart was pounding against his chest, but he hunched his shoulders in what he hoped was a casual shrug. "Maybe at the research facility or . . . or on that tour."

"So!" Dad released Justin abruptly. "And how many others have overheard classified information from office big mouths?"

He paced around the room, his fingers working through his rusty curls. Justin scooted back to keep out of his way. He and Jenny exchanged nervous glances. They had never seen their father so angry.

Dad's gaze suddenly fell on their apprehensive faces. He stopped and let out a quiet sigh. "Well, what's done is done."

He gave them a stern look. "Justin—Jenny, I want you to forget you ever heard this conversation. And, son, if you remember where you got that information, let me know right away."

Justin nodded miserably. Dad strode out of the living room

"Hey!" Jenny wailed as the door slammed shut behind him. "What about my sundae?" But she said it softly. Justin escaped to his bedroom before she asked him any more questions. Scrambling into his pajamas, he crawled into bed and turned off the light, although it was still early.

He was stretched out on his bed, staring up into the darkness, when he heard the ta-tat, ta-tat that was the twins' special signal. Ignoring the knock, he rolled over and closed his eyes. After a moment, the door creaked open.

"Justin? Are you awake?" Jenny whispered.

Justin lay still, breathing in and out in the deep, even rhythm of a sleeping person. At last, he heard a sigh and the soft closing of the door. Justin rolled over. The spy business had somehow lost its appeal.

If only he hadn't asked his father about the invisibility shield! He'd found out what he wanted, but now he'd had to lie to his dad as well as his sister. At least he'd gotten Grady the information he needed. Before long, the traitors would be arrested, and his life could go back to normal.

Justin sat up in bed with a jerk. What did God think of his lying to his father and sister? That was something he hadn't thought about until now. Hadn't he read somewhere in the Bible that lying was one of the things God hated most?

But this is different! he argued with himself. *I can't tell them the truth—not if I'm going to prove Dad's innocent. I'm sure God will understand.* Pulling the bedclothes up over his head, he squeezed his eyes shut. And for the first time since he could remember, he went to sleep without praying.

At breakfast, Dad, who had been so relaxed and carefree with the completion of his project, was preoccupied, his freckled face stern. Jenny's thoughtful glances told Justin she hadn't forgotten his behavior of the day before.

Shoving away his half-eaten breakfast, Dad looked across the table. "Justin, did you ever remember where you overheard the information you mentioned last night?"

Justin choked on a bite of toast. Grabbing for his juice glass, he gulped half its contents before he could answer. "Uh, no. I hadn't really thought about it."

Pushing back his chair, Ron Parker stood up. He leaned over to kiss his wife. "I'm going to the office, honey. I should be back in plenty of time for supper."

Mom protested gently. "I thought you had the day off!"

"So did I!" Dad said. "But something unexpected has come up."

Jenny glanced at her brother. Justin knew by the look in her eye that he was in for it the minute she got him alone. As soon as he was excused from the table, he snatched up his backpack and headed at a run for the bus stop.

By the time Jenny panted up behind him, the bus was pulling into the curb. Scrambling aboard, he looked around for a seat that already held one other person. But it wasn't so easy. All the occupied seats already held two passengers, and he was forced to take an empty one. Jenny plopped down beside him.

She twisted around to face her brother. "Look, Justin, I won't bug you anymore about skipping that class if you'll tell me what's going on. What was all that 'invisibility' stuff last night? And why is Dad so worried about it?"

"How would *I* know?" Justin growled. "I was just asking some questions!" Dragging out his notes for the day's history test, he pretended to study. "Why don't you ask Dad if you're so bent on finding out?"

"Justin, you make me so mad!" Picking up her books, Jenny flounced over to an empty seat. Justin glanced after her, then shrugged and flipped over a sheet of notes on the Civil War.

But though he kept his eyes fastened on the page, he kept seeing his father's worried face. His earlier excitement over working with a real secret agent now seemed childish, and he wished fervently that he'd never seen Grady. If he hadn't been so eager to uncover a mystery that day on Deer Island, none of this would have ever happened!

No, that wasn't quite true. His father and the GP145 would still be in trouble, even if he didn't know about it. Justin slammed his notebook shut. If only he could talk to Dad!

Grady had ordered Justin not to talk. He'd said that it would ruin the operation. But if someone really *had* given Dad those computer CDs to pass on to Abdul, then his father could pinpoint Grady's traitor in a minute. Why couldn't Grady see that?

Grady was concerned that Justin's father might accidentally let information slip to Abdul or to the Boeing traitor, but the sandy-haired agent didn't know Dad. Ron Parker would never let the traitors suspect he knew of their activities.

I know I promised not to tell! But if it means catching the spies before they can get the invisibility shield—? That question came between Justin and his studies all day, and he didn't have to wait for the return of his history exam to know that he'd flunked his second test!

Mom had warmed supper over for the second time when Justin finally heard his father's car turn into the driveway that evening. He knew something was wrong the moment Dad walked into the kitchen. Jenny took the words out of his mouth. "Hey, Dad! What happened?"

Dad set down his briefcase, his freckled face grim. "There was a break-in at the research facility last night."

"Oh, dear!" Mom set a plate of dried-out pork chops on the table. "Did anyone get hurt?"

Dad shook his head. "It wasn't that kind of break-in. Someone got into the Boeing mainframe computer. It was about ten o'clock last night according to the computer logs. None of our own computer terminals were used, so it had to be someone on the outside."

Justin knew what his father meant. Someone had patched his own computer into the Boeing mainframe computer by modem, a device that allowed a computer to transmit data to another computer over telephone lines.

"Whoever broke in was an expert," Dad went on. "The mainframe computer has a built-in security system. But the thief made it clear into the classified data banks before the alarm went off."

Justin listened, troubled. The break-in was too much of a coincidence to hope that it wasn't connected to his father's project. The Boeing traitor already had inside access to the invisibility shield. But Islamic terrorists had tried once before to get the shield without paying. Could they too have found out that the project was finished?

"Well, I'm sure it didn't have anything to do with what *I* heard!" he burst out. He broke off as three pairs of eyes stared at him in surprise. *Well, it didn't!* he told himself stubbornly. After all, he'd gotten that information from Grady. With a puzzled look at Justin, Dad continued his explanation of the break-in.

"He was interested in top secret government projects. At least that's where he ended up. He didn't get far enough into the data banks to tell us which project he was after."

Glancing around at his family's anxious faces, Dad forced a smile. "Don't worry. I set up the safeguards myself. The best computer hacker in the world couldn't break into those data banks without the proper passwords."

And if he's one of the guys who knows the passwords? The GP145 might be safe from outside access, but with the project finished, that inside traitor could be stealing the plans for the invisibility shield right now! Justin suddenly made up his mind. Grady or no Grady, his father *had* to know that his project was in danger.

After supper, Dad stretched out in his favorite armchair in the living room. Justin waited until his mother and sister were out of the room before he dropped his computer magazine. "Dad, there's something I've got to tell . . ."

The sharp buzz of the doorbell interrupted his confession. Annoyed, he jumped to his feet. "I'll get it, Dad."

The bell buzzed again. Justin yanked open the front door. "Just a m . . . m . . ."

He broke off, his mouth frozen open in shock. Only once before—and then at a distance—had he seen the strange figure who now stood on the Parkers' front steps. But he recognized the man in long, flowing white robes and a checkered headdress.

"Ab . . . Abdul!" Justin clutched at the doorknob to support his suddenly shaky legs. What was the Arab terrorist doing here? Had he somehow guessed that Justin knew his true identity?

But there was only friendliness in the piercing, black eyes. "Abdul el Kutub at your service," he said politely. Abdul spoke with a slight British accent. "You must be Justin. Your father has spoken much about you."

The Arab visitor extended his hand. Justin put out his own hand with reluctance.

But he didn't have to say anything. Dad was already at his side. "Abdul! When did you fly in?"

"Just this afternoon." Gripping Dad by the shoulders, Abdul kissed him soundly on both cheeks in a traditional Middle Eastern greeting. "Your office told me you'd already left for home. I hoped I might catch you here."

"I'm glad you did." Dad swung the door open wide, beaming his pleasure. "Come on in."

Abdul swept into the living room, his white robes flapping. At the sound of voices, Mom and Jenny hurried into the living room. Dad introduced his wife.

"Happy to meet you," Mom said. "Your English is very good."

The man flashed a smile. "I have studied in England. My father wished me to bring the benefits of your Western technology to my country."

"Abdul's being modest," Dad interrupted. "He has a master's

degree in engineering and has studied computer science in both Paris and the United States."

Computer science? Whoever had broken into Boeing had been an expert in computer science. Justin eyed the visitor with new interest. Abdul was now smiling down at Jenny.

"You must be Jenny. I have heard much about you." He glanced across at Dad. "You were right, Ron. She is as beautiful as my own daughter."

Jenny went pink with pleasure. Justin smoldered. Couldn't anyone in his family but him see what kind of man this Abdul really was?

He studied Abdul el Kutub. He had to admit the guy didn't look like a terrorist or spy. But . . . Justin glowered at the visitor. He could at least read the man's true nature behind the piercing, dark gaze and that flaring, hawklike nose.

Dad ushered his friend to a seat. "So what's brought you stateside, Abdul? We didn't expect you for another couple of weeks."

Abdul sank into a chair. "I had to change my plans. Something unexpected came up."

Like the news that Dad's project is finished, Justin thought sarcastically.

Abdul turned to Dad. "Ron, this is not entirely a social call. I need to speak with you."

"Sure! We'll just step into my office." The ring of the telephone cut him off. Dad got to his feet.

"If you'll excuse me a moment, Abdul. I'm expecting a call." Dad hurried into the kitchen. Justin debated whether or not he should go after him.

He brought his attention back to their visitor. "It is called a *kaffiyeh*," Abdul was telling Jenny, indicating the checkered headdress. "Though I have studied several years abroad, my father expects me to dress like my people, even when I'm a visitor in your country."

Abdul's keen, dark gaze moved from Jenny to Justin. "Perhaps you two would like to visit my country someday. I have a son and daughter of my own very close to your age. They would love to meet you."

Jenny's brown eyes glowed. "That would be great! Justin and I love visiting new countries."

Justin scowled. The nerve of this guy! And Jenny was falling for every word.

"No, we don't!" he said loudly. Shooting the Arab a dark look, he added meaningfully, "I'm completely loyal to good old America!"

But to his disappointment, he could detect no hint of guilt or understanding on Abdul's face. The visitor looked puzzled. Justin glanced at his sister. She stared at him with incredulous eyes.

Dad was back in the room before Justin could say anything else. "If you'd like to step down to the office, Abdul, we'll take care of that business."

Jenny waited only until the door to the basement had closed behind the two men before turning on her brother. "Justin, how could you be so rude? He was just trying to be nice!"

Her expression softened as she studied her brother, and she said gently, "What's gotten into you, Justin? You've been acting weird all week."

Justin was already feeling ashamed of his rudeness. Grady had forbidden him to talk to his father for fear the NSA investigation would get back to Abdul. And now *he* had done his best to rouse the enemy's suspicions! But he protested weakly. "Jenny, he isn't the nice guy you all think!"

"What are you talking about?" Jenny was angry now. "He's Dad's friend, isn't he? Just because he's Arab . . ."

"It isn't that!" Justin stopped, unable to explain further. He finished lamely, "I just have a bad feeling about him."

"Well, *I'm* starting to get a bad feeling about you!" Jenny retorted, and she stomped down the hall to her bedroom.

Throwing himself into an armchair, Justin kicked his feet restlessly. What could Abdul want to talk to his father about?

Justin made up his mind. He really should know what that man was doing here. Crossing the living room, he cracked open the door leading to the basement. Pulling off his shoes, Justin slipped through the opening. He eased the door shut, then crept stealthily down the stairs in his stocking feet.

At the bottom of the stairs, he peered around the wall that formed one side of the stairway. The recreation room was empty, but at the far end, the door of the office stood cracked open. Moving silently across the basement, he peeped through the gap.

Dad's back was to the door, but Justin could hear the earnest murmur of his familiar voice. Abdul was nodding agreement, his dark gaze intent on what Dad was saying. But though Justin strained his ears, he couldn't make out the topic of conversation.

Justin's shoulders slumped with disappointment. Just then the two men rose to their feet and turned toward the door. His eyes widened with dismay as Dad pulled a computer disc from his shirt pocket and handed it to Abdul.

No! Justin's hand went to the doorknob. *I've got to tell Dad about Abdul right now! He can't hand that information over. It might even be the invisibility shield!*

But before he could push open the door, he heard his father's voice, clearly now that the two men were facing the door. "Yes, I had some trouble getting the data from the mainframe computer, but it's all there now."

Justin stiffened with shock. Dad couldn't mean what he'd just said! But his father was still speaking. "That's the last installment of that data we discussed, Abdul. I'll let you know when I have more."

The Arab's reply was too low to catch, but Dad shook his head. "No, I haven't talked to my family. I didn't want to upset them just yet, especially the twins. But it will certainly be a pleasure to work with you, Abdul. I've always wanted to see the Middle East."

Justin didn't wait to hear more. He dashed across the basement and up the stairs. There was no point in talking to his father now. No mysterious traitor had conned Dad into handing over those computer CDs. It was Dad himself who was leaking classified information to Abdul!

Justin caught his breath, horrified. Innocently or not, his father was working for the enemies of the United States of America!

Chapter Seven

THE SECRET SEARCH

Justin made his way unseen to his room. Again, he lay sleepless far into the night. His head was beginning to ache. Nothing made sense. He knew his father! No matter what he had heard and seen, there had to be a logical explanation for those CDs.

Justin turned over, his sheet twisting like a straitjacket around his legs.

If I was really patriotic, like Grady said, I'd tell him about Abdul, he thought dully, rolling over to untangle himself. He still had the government agent's beeper number. But he had no intention of adding any more evidence to the National Security Agency's case against his father. Justin knew his father was innocent, but even he could see how easy it would be for a jury to believe otherwise.

When at last he fell into an uneasy sleep, he was haunted by dreams of his father standing before a jury of unsmiling military officers. "Guilty!" they chorused, pointing accusing fingers at a bewildered Ron Parker.

The first dull light of a rainy morning was creeping over the windowsill as Justin pulled himself out of bed. The house was still silent. Justin washed his face and made his way out to the kitchen. He was sitting alone at the table, staring into a cup of hot chocolate when his father walked in.

"Hi, Dad!" Justin jumped to his feet. "Did you sleep well?"

But his forced cheerfulness didn't fool his father. Sliding into a chair, Dad leaned his elbows on the table. He gave his son a keen look. "What's bothering you, Justin?"

"What'd you mean?" Justin glanced up indignantly. "Has Jenny been talking to you?"

Dad's eyebrows rose. "No. Should she?"

He added gently, "I don't need your sister to tell me when something's bothering you, Justin. You've been moping all week."

Dad reached over and gave him a quick hug. "Son, we've always been able to talk. Why don't you tell me what's wrong?"

A lump rose in Justin's throat at his father's tenderness, but he managed to keep his own voice steady. "Nothing's wrong, Dad. Just a lot of homework; that's all."

"If you're still worried about that information you over-heard . . ."

Justin gave a quick shake of his head. "No, Dad! I'm sure it didn't mean anything." Grabbing for his cocoa, he took a hasty swallow. It was still scalding hot, but he gulped it down, ignoring the troubled look in his father's eyes, then escaped to his room.

The rain clouds had drifted away by midafternoon. Justin was just finishing soccer practice when a shrill whistle brought his head around. He let out a deep sigh of relief. He hadn't realized how worried he'd actually been until he saw Grady O'Brian standing outside the chain-link fence.

Justin hurried across the field. He'd asked Grady to let him know when his father was cleared of the espionage charges. If that was why the secret agent was here, then the traitor must now be under arrest. Maybe that conversation with Abdul last night hadn't meant anything after all.

"Have you caught him?" he demanded eagerly when he reached the fence.

But the secret agent didn't have a look of someone bringing good news. His face was lined with weariness. His expression was grave, and Justin had a sudden sinking feeling that more trouble was ahead.

"I'm afraid not," Grady admitted. "But I think we're close. Just hang in there a little longer."

Justin caught his breath. "The break-in at Dad's office! That really was someone trying to steal the invisibility shield, wasn't it?"

"Shhh!" Grady cast a quick glance up and down the street. "So you know about the break-in. I need your help, badly!"

"Sure!" Justin squared his shoulders. "What'd you want me to do?"

Stepping closer to the fence, Grady lowered his voice. "I've got to get into the Boeing computer. I need access to the GP145 data files."

"The data files!" Justin repeated blankly. "But, what for?"

The government agent hesitated, then explained, "We found out yesterday that Abdul is back in the country. And you know what he's here for! He won't leave the country without that invisibility shield."

Justin gave a wary nod. Did Grady know that the Arab had been at the Parkers' home last night? He must, but Justin wasn't going to bring it up if he didn't have to. Last night, he'd been afraid that his father was somehow involved in passing on the plans for the invisibility shield. But Dad had been worried about the safety of his present project. Whatever information he had copied for Abdul el Kutub, it couldn't be the GP145. Abdul must be working with more than one person at Boeing.

He brought his attention back to Grady. The government agent's gray eyes were somber. "Our traitor will be making his move any time," he said. "We've learned that Abdul and his terrorist pals aren't just out to steal our military's latest invention. They want to destroy it, so that they alone will have access to that technology. The instant Abdul gets his hands on that invisibility shield, his accomplice has orders to destroy the original GP145 file."

Justin's stomach gave a sickening lurch. "So why don't you arrest Abdul?" he demanded. "I mean, if you know all that!"

Grady shook his head. "No, we'll just have to wait. I've got men tailing Abdul. The instant he meets with his contact at Boeing, we'll have our traitor with the evidence in hand, and we'll arrest them both. But if they first manage to destroy the computer files of the project, our country's defense will be set back for years! That's why we need to get into the GP145 files— to secure a copy of the plans before we move in on Abdul."

"So why don't you just warn Boeing, so they can put a copy somewhere sa—Oh, I get it!" Justin snapped his fingers. "You're afraid the traitor will find out."

"That's right, Justin," Grady said. "Whoever our traitor is, he holds a very high position at the research facility. Odds are, we'd end up warning the very person we're after. Justin, we're running out of time. We've got to get into those data banks right away!"

Justin frowned. "So what do you want with me? I'm no computer expert!"

"But your father is. He can get us into those data banks. In fact, your father is one of the few men whose password gives access to the entire GP145 file. That's why we need your help, Justin."

Justin's mouth dropped open as it dawned on him what Grady wanted him to do. "You want the password my dad uses to get into the Boeing computers?" he demanded incredulously. "But I don't know his password. And he's sure not going to tell *me* what it is! He says it's very important to keep it secret."

"Don't ask him. Search for it!" Grady ordered. "You're his son. You must have some idea where he would write down something like that."

Justin studied his shoes. Lying to his dad had been bad enough, but to steal his password? He shook his head slowly. "I don't think I can do that, Grady. My dad trusts me."

There was a silence. Justin raised his eyes. Grady's features were stern and hard, and the steel-gray eyes were as cold as Puget Sound.

"Haven't you heard what I've been saying, Justin?" His voice was as icy as his eyes. "Maybe you're forgetting that all I've got to do is pick up the phone and say that your father's our man, after all, and NSA agents will be at your front door within the hour."

Justin was suddenly angry. "What are you trying to say?" he demanded. "That if I don't get that password, you'll arrest my dad?"

Grady softened his voice. "I'm not trying to threaten you,

Justin. What I'm saying is that your father would have been arrested long ago if it weren't for me. The least you can do is give me a little cooperation."

The stern line of his mouth tightened. "Justin, if you don't help us, we'll be forced to bring our investigation out into the open to prevent losing the GP145 altogether. If we don't catch Abdul's accomplice with the evidence in his hand, my superiors will never believe your father is innocent."

There was no mistaking the urgency in Grady's voice. Justin weakened. "It's just that I feel awful doing this to my dad. But if it's that important, well . . . I can't promise anything, but I'll do my best."

"That's all I'm asking. When you get the password, call me on the beeper. I'll be waiting."

Grady hurried down the sidewalk. Resting his forehead against the metal links of the fence, Justin watched the secret agent disappear around a corner. *How am I ever going to find that password? It could be anywhere!*

The sudden gunning of an engine jerked his thoughts back to his surroundings. Raising his head, he saw a brown van edge away from the curb across the street. Wasn't that the van he'd seen down near Grady's apartment?

The van moved slowly past the playing field. The driver was a slim man with an olive-skinned complexion and curly black hair. Justin's eyes sharpened with interest as he caught sight of a streak of orange across the side of the van. Yes, that was the van he'd seen! Justin grinned. The owner clearly hadn't discovered the paint job before it dried.

He returned to his own problem. Dad must keep his password

written down somewhere. He wouldn't risk forgetting something as important as that.

Well, if it was written down, it had to be at home. He would just have to search the house—but not while anyone was home to ask questions.

"Hey, Justin! Who was that man you were talking to?"

Justin jumped. He hadn't even heard his sister approaching. "What man?" he evaded, swinging around to face her.

"You know who I'm talking about. I was watching you from soccer practice." Jenny pointed with her chin toward the far side of the field where the girls' team had been practicing.

When her brother only shrugged, she persisted, "Come on, Justin, I'm not stupid. Why are you keeping such a big secret? Are you . . . I mean . . . you're not doing something wrong?"

"Nothing's wrong!" he exploded. "Can't you just leave me alone?"

There was a long silence. Justin looked every direction but at his sister. Then Jenny said in a small voice, "Justin, aren't we friends anymore?"

Something twisted inside him, but he kept his eyes stubbornly fixed on the school buildings. There would be time when this was all over to make up with Jenny. Until then, the farther she stayed away from him the better.

Justin didn't dare risk skipping classes again the next day, but during his pre-lunch study hall he headed for home. Mom would be at the Emergency Center until early afternoon, leaving him plenty of time to search the house for Dad's password.

Stepping into the living room, he stood listening for a moment. It had been a long time since he'd come home to an empty house. For no reason, his heart began to race.

Shaking off his unease, he headed down the hall to his parents' bedroom. A computer sat on top of the desk on the far side of the king-sized waterbed. Dad often worked from this desk, and Justin had already decided that it was the most logical place to look for his father's password.

He searched through the desk drawers. There were a few memos and receipts scribbled with his father's sloppy handwriting, but nothing that resembled a computer password.

He'd finished the last drawer when he remembered something he'd read in a recent detective story. Pulling out all the desk drawers, he felt carefully along the inside of the cavities he had created. But he found nothing there or taped to the bottom of the drawers. He tidied up the mess he'd made, then searched the rest of the room; from his mother's jewelry box to the inside of his father's shoes.

Admitting defeat at last, Justin walked over to the window. Leaning his elbows on the sill, he rested his chin in his hands and stared gloomily across the frostbitten flower beds of the front lawn. Where could Dad have hidden a scrap of paper with a word or two written on it? He'd have to hide it where it wouldn't be thrown out by accident. That ruled out most of the other rooms of the house. Or did it?

Suddenly he stiffened, all thoughts of the password flying out of his mind. A brown van was parked across the street and down three houses! A man stepped out from the shelter of the oak tree—a slim man with black, curly hair!

Justin backed away from the window. That van again! This was too much for coincidence. Who *was* that man out there? Grady had said he was going to assign someone to protect Dad. Maybe this was one of his agents.

But . . . Grady had also said that someone was after him! What if this man were one of the Islamic terrorists who had tried to kidnap Dad?

Justin locked the front door, then peered out the window. The van driver was climbing back into the van. He relaxed. If the guy was just watching the house, then he must be one of Grady's men.

He suddenly wished he wasn't alone in that big, empty house. Justin headed for the basement stairs. Mom's office was the only other place he could imagine his father filing a copy of his password. Closing the office door behind him, Justin concentrated on giving the small room a thorough search.

Except for two armchairs, there was nothing in the office but his mother's computer desk and a small metal filing cabinet. Justin looked through the desk, then removed the drawers and ran his fingers across the inside of the frame. Nothing! Turning to the metal cabinet, he leafed quickly through each file. But he found only papers.

He was fitting the last file back into the cabinet when his hands stiffened on the folder of loose papers. He held his breath as he heard the sound of footsteps walking across the living room floor overhead. Someone was in the house!

Justin threw a frantic glance around the small office. There was no place to hide in here. But as he started for the door, he heard the distinct creak of a foot on the first step of the basement stairs. Diving under the desk, he squeezed as far back as possible, then pulled his mother's office chair in behind him.

Don't come down here! His mind set up a desperate refrain as though he could will the intruder away.

The creaking stopped. Justin strained his ears, but he could hear nothing but the thunder of his own heart. After a long moment, he let out a slow breath of relief and scrambled out from his hiding place. Password or no password, he wasn't going to stay alone in this house any longer!

He was halfway across the small stretch of carpet when he froze in midstep.

Silently, stealthily, the doorknob was turning!

Chapter Eight

CODE CRACKING

Justin glanced around the small office. There had to be something in here that would serve as a weapon! His eyes fell on his mother's dictionary. He grabbed the heavy volume, then ducked behind the door.

The door swung open. Justin raised the dictionary over his head. But the book slid from his fingers as he recognized the slim figure that slipped into the room.

"Jenny!" He collapsed with relief against the wall. "What are you doing here?"

His sister's eyes narrowed. "What are *you* doing here? I looked for you at lunch. One of the kids told me he'd seen you getting on the bus. Justin, what's going on?"

"Never mind that,'" Justin said urgently. "Did you see a brown van outside?"

"The only van I saw was driving away." Jenny glared at her brother. "I don't know what's gotten into you! You've skipped school and lied to practically everyone!"

She reached for the phone. "I'm calling Mom and Dad right now."

"No, please don't call!" Justin grabbed her wrist. "I'm not

doing anything wrong, I promise. In fact, it . . . it's very important for all of us."

Jenny thawed a little. "I suppose you've gotten mixed up in another mystery," she said, letting the receiver fall back into its cradle. "But why won't you tell me what's going on? We've never kept secrets from each other before."

"I can't." Justin released her wrist. "Please, Jenny. In a couple more days everything will work out."

"Well, okay," Jenny agreed reluctantly. "Two more days. But you'd better have a pretty good excuse."

She started back across the basement. "Come on. We'd better get back to school before Mrs. Meyer misses her 'star' student again and calls Mom and Dad *for* me."

Justin followed her upstairs. The brown van was gone. Whoever the driver had been, Jenny's arrival must have scared him off. Jenny was right—they might as well get back to school. If Dad's password was written down, it was too well hidden for him to find. He'd have to get the information Grady wanted another way. And he'd just had an idea how to go about it.

That evening Dad was stretched out in his easy chair with a new computer magazine. Justin longed to ask him if there had been any more trouble at the research facility, but he didn't want his father to connect the subject with his other questions.

"Dad, I've got a problem." Pasting a cheerful expression on his face, Justin dropped to the carpet beside Dad's chair. He could see his sister perk up across the room, but that couldn't be helped now. "Could you give me some computer advice?"

Dad lowered his magazine. He looked so pleased that Justin felt vaguely ashamed. "Of course, son. What kind of a problem?"

"Well, I'm working on this computer project at school. I'd almost finished when someone got into the computer and messed up my file."

This, at least, was true. The school bullies, the Devlon cousins, had in fact accessed his project. But he'd been too worried about his father to really care. "I've put it back together. But how can I keep them from messing it up again?"

Dad grinned down at him. "You just need to set up some safeguards so you're the only one with access to your file."

"You mean, like you do for your projects at Boeing?" Justin leaned forward, his freckled face eager. "You said no one could get into the data banks without the right password. Could I do something like that?"

"Sure. You'll just have to program the computer to give access to your files only after a certain password has been typed in."

"So how would I pick a password?" Justin asked. "It can't be just anything, can it?"

"You're best off to keep it simple. Use just one password for all the files you want to keep private. And make sure it's something you're not likely to forget, or you'll find yourself locked out of your own programs!"

The conversation was going exactly as Justin had hoped. He latched on to his father's last statement. "So what if I do forget it? What do you do, Dad, when you forget your password? Keep it written down somewhere in case of emergency?"

Justin held his breath, afraid that this time he'd gone too far. But Dad only laughed and said, "I've found it safer never to write down a password. If I keep it where I can find it, so can someone else. So I've developed my own method of remembering my password."

Dad gave him a quizzical look. "Exactly how secret did you want to keep this file?"

"Oh, very secret!" Justin assured his father. "Could you help me make my files as safe as yours?"

Dad went on, "The hardest password to break is a combination of numbers. But it's also the hardest to remember, especially if you're always having to change your password as I do."

Justin sat up straight at this. "You mean, you don't always keep the same password? But why not?"

"It's standard security, son. At Boeing, we change all our passwords every couple months. It lessens the possibility of someone breaking into the data banks—as happened the other night."

Justin tried to hide his disappointment. "But . . . then how would you ever remember which password you're using right now?"

Dad pulled a pen from his shirt pocket and turned over the back of the computer magazine. "Take the last date something important happened to you. Maybe a big ball game, a test, whatever. Here, give me a date!"

"How about that last ball game we won?" Justin calculated backward. "It was two weeks ago—November 2."

"So you'd have the numbers 11 and 2." Dad wrote the date on the back of the magazine. "Now just so it doesn't look so much like a date, reverse your numbers—211—and you've got your password."

Justin scribbled the numbers down for himself. He frowned. "It still looks a lot like a date. What if someone guesses your system?"

"So multiply it by another number. Better yet—two, " Dad said absently turning back to his computer magazine. "Just keep it simple so you don't forget it. Something like, say, the days in a week—number seven—times your birth month. You'll end up with what looks like random numbers. And it's a pretty safe system since no one else knows what you consider the last significant day in your life."

No one but your own family! Justin stared at the scribbled numbers. This had to be Dad's own system. And if it was, he was sure he knew exactly what his father's password was!

"Thanks a million, Dad." Jumping to his feet, Justin gave his father a hard hug. "You don't know how much this means to me!"

Dad looked surprised at this unusual gesture, but he nodded. "Any time, son. Let me know if you have any problem setting up the program."

All that remained for Justin now was to call Grady's beeper number, but he suddenly felt guilty. Once again, he'd used his relationship with his father to obtain secret information.

Justin slipped downstairs to the phone, but he hesitated a long time before he picked up the receiver. He knew well the value of the information he had. That password could get a user into far more than just the one file Grady needed. And while Justin trusted Grady, he hadn't liked the looks of his sidekick, Hacker.

But we've got to get that spy! He had to make a decision. Taking a deep breath, he dialed Grady's beeper number. He'd hardly hung up when the phone rang. He grabbed for the receiver. It was Grady.

"You've got the password?"

"I think so," Justin answered.

"Good work, kid!" Grady's voice warmed with approval. "Okay, let's have it."

Justin hesitated again before he spoke. "I . . . I can't give it to you, Grady. I'm sorry."

"You *what?*" There was a strangled sound on the other end of the line. "Justin, we've already gone through this! We need those files now!"

"Wait!" Justin broke in hurriedly. "I'll help you get into the files. But . . . but I'll have to type in the password myself."

To his relief, Grady sounded more amused than angry. "Okay, Justin, meet me at the apartment first thing in the morning. One way or another, this is all going to be over tomorrow."

"I've got to go downtown this morning," Justin told his sister when they hurried to catch the bus the next morning. "But this is the very last time, I promise," he added hastily as Jenny's face clouded over.

He remembered Grady's last words. "In fact, everything should be all over by tonight. Then you'll see how important this all is."

Jenny didn't bother arguing. Instead, she changed the subject. "Hey, Justin, why don't you like Abdul el Kutub? He seems like such a nice guy."

"He's a spy!" Justin retorted hotly, then clapped his hand over his mouth. But she only nodded thoughtfully and asked no further questions.

Jenny swung aboard the bus that would take her to the junior high, but Justin waited for one heading in the direction of Grady's apartment. He reached the building but stopped short when he saw the brown van parked across the street. *Not again!*

But this van was freshly painted and shining with wax. He'd just decided he had the wrong vehicle when he caught sight of a slim man with black, curly hair walking down the front steps of the apartment building.

Justin relaxed. So this *was* the right van—with a new paint job. If the driver was coming from the apartment, then he must be one of Grady's agents, after all.

He made his way up to the third-floor apartment. He hadn't knocked but Grady yanked the door open. "We've got to move fast!"

Hacker was bent over the computer. "Okay, kid!" he snapped, without looking up. "Spit out the password!"

"I'll type it in myself," Justin told him firmly. He glanced up at Grady, and the sandy-haired agent nodded.

Hacker only grunted. He bent over the keyboard. "I can get us in as far as the other night. Then it's up to the kid."

"The other night! What do you mean?" Justin straightened up with a jerk. He stared from the computer operator to Grady. "You mean, you guys were the ones who tried to break into Boeing the other night? But . . . you said it was someone trying to steal Dad's project."

"I saw no need to keep you informed of everything that's been going on," the government agent explained crisply. "But, yes, we did try to get into the Boeing computers—to do exactly what we're doing now, and for the same reasons. You don't really think we would have asked you to get that password for us until we'd tried every other possible way of checking those files."

Grady gave Hacker a sour look. "Only our computer expert here fouled it up and set off the security alarm."

Hacker ignored the comment. But before Justin could slide into the chair Hacker had vacated, the computer screen went blank. The computer began issuing a warning beep, and a strange pattern blossomed in the middle of the screen.

"Turn it off! They're searching for our computer!" Pushing Justin out of the way, Hacker stabbed at a switch. The computer blinked off.

"What's going on?" Grady stared at the empty computer screen. "Why'd it go blank?"

"They've put a block on the mainframe computer. No outside calls. We can't get in now even with the password," Hacker explained, his narrow face sullen. "And if you modem in, like we did, they trace the line back to locate the computer that's trying to access."

He slammed his hand down on the computer desk. "In other words, we're finished. The only way into those data banks now is at the source itself."

Grady cut Hacker off with a wave of his hand. His square features were thoughtful. "So, the only access into the data banks is at the source. Does that mean you could get into those files from inside the research facility?"

"Sure!" Hacker said. "Every computer terminal in the building's linked to the mainframe. But the security's tighter getting into the building than it is over the phone lines."

Ignoring Hacker's last comment, Grady said softly, "Including the terminal in Ron Parker's office?" Hacker's pale eyes suddenly narrowed. Both men turned to look at Justin.

"Me?" Justin took a step backward. "But . . . but I don't know anything about that computer!"

"There's nothing to it, Justin—once you're inside. Hacker here will tell you exactly how to get into those files." Grady jerked his head toward the computer operator. "Hacker, get over here and tell the kid what to do."

Justin didn't care for the smile with which Hacker reached into a desk drawer and pulled out two CD-Rs, one silver and the other gold. "The silver is for making a copy of the files. I assume any kid of Parker's knows enough to do that much."

Hacker ripped a sheet from a pad of note paper and scrawled across it. "Just follow these directions. They'll get you into the system."

Picking up the gold CD-R, he went on, "Don't put this one in until you've made your copy."

Breaking off, Hacker glanced at Grady who quickly explained, "The only way our traitor can get the GP145 is to do what we're doing now—copy the plans from the mainframe computer data banks. And the computer records every addition, deletion, or copy made of a file."

Grady nodded toward the gold disc. "That disk holds a special program Hacker has made up. It'll check the data banks for any unauthorized copies of computer files. The program can tell us exactly which office terminal and which password has been used to get in the data banks. That should give us a lead on our traitor."

Uh-oh! A program that checked the computer log for un-

authorized copies? Justin remembered his father handing a computer disk to Abdul.

"Uh, Grady," he said hesitantly. "What if there isn't any traitor in Boeing? What if Abdul's been getting that stuff from someone innocent?"

Hacker gave a short bark of laughter. "What's the matter, kid?" he sneered. "Worried that your father isn't so innocent, after all?"

"Of course not!" Justin retorted. "It's just that I've met the people my dad works with. They all seem like pretty nice guys."

Grady slid the two CDs into a black pouch. "Look, kid. If you can get the GP145 file for us before Abdul or someone else manages to destroy it, I'll guarantee the NSA will forget about your father—whether he's innocent or not."

Justin nodded, then Grady clapped him on the back. "By tonight everything will be all over, and Abdul will be in custody. But first we need you to get us a copy of that file. If not for your country, then do it for your father!"

With reluctance, Justin took the pouch from Grady. "But what about my dad? He'll be in the office."

"No problem." Grady picked up the phone. "I'll make a call that will get him out of his office for an hour or two. You just think of a good excuse to get in there."

The government agent began punching in numbers. Shoving the black pouch inside his jacket, Justin wandered across the room and looked out the window. The brown van was still sitting across the street. The curly-haired driver was sitting behind the wheel, but as Justin watched, he opened the door and stepped down.

"Hey, Grady!" Justin called. "That man in the brown van.

Who is he? And why has he been following me instead of my dad?"

"What man?" Slamming down the phone, Grady strode rapidly to Justin's side.

"That man!" Justin pointed as the driver walked around to the back of the van.

The driver opened the back doors and four men climbed out. All five walked toward the apartment building. Grady's hand bit into Justin's shoulder. "Where have you seen that man before?"

"Well, I saw the van last time I came . . . then at school when you were there . . . and outside my house." Justin's voice faltered. "You mean, he isn't working for you? But I saw him coming out of this building!"

Grady didn't answer. Yanking open the drawers of the desk, the government agent began stuffing papers into a small briefcase. "Hacker, they've found us! Clear that computer!"

Glancing at the screen, Justin saw that Hacker was deleting file after file from the computer. It took only moments. Not even bothering to switch off the computer, Hacker started toward the door. Grady grabbed the briefcase in one hand and Justin's arm in the other. "Let's get out of here!"

But it was too late! Already Justin heard the sound of running feet in the hall. A moment later, a hard fist pounded at the apartment door.

Chapter Nine

ACCESS DENIED

The two men looked at each other. Then, as though they'd exchanged a signal, they turned on their heels and headed for the bedroom, Grady herding Justin ahead of him.

Grady locked the bedroom door, propping a chair under the doorknob. Hacker was already scrambling out the window. Throwing a leg over the sill, Justin followed him onto a rusty fire escape. Behind him, he could hear shouts and heavy blows on the apartment door. Grady was climbing out when Justin heard a crash. The front door!

"Who are those guys?" Justin found breath to ask as they clattered down the fire stairs. "Do they work for Abdul?"

"Yes!" Grady's square features were grim. "And they're after me, not you or your dad. I don't know how they found me, but they're not likely to be too pleasant if they catch up to us."

Justin heard another crash. Abdul's men must be in the bedroom! Justin quickened his pace, taking the rusty metal stairs two and three at a time. He had just reached the alley when he heard the faint scrape of a window being raised.

Justin had wondered why the agent parked his car in such an out-of-the-way spot. Now he knew. He danced with impatience as Grady unlocked the sedan. Already he could hear a clattering on the metal staircase above him.

Grady yanked open the back car door. Hacker climbed into the passenger side. "Get in and keep that red hair of yours down," he ordered crisply.

But it was too late for that. Justin was tumbling into the backseat when a voice shouted, "Hey, that's the Parker kid!" Glancing up, he saw a man leaning over the metal banister one flight above. He had a gun!

The van driver clattered downstairs with two of his men at his heels, but Grady had wasted no time. By the time the three men reached the ground, the sedan was racing out of the alley.

Justin, kneeling on the backseat, saw the van driver drop to a crouch behind them. His eyes widened in alarm as the man raised his gun to aim at the back of the sedan. But before Justin could even duck, the van driver lowered his weapon. Waving for the others to follow, he ran after the sedan.

The car was already rounding the front of the building, tires screeching on the corner. Grady sped down the long, straight street that ran between the dingy brick buildings of the housing development. Justin watched the five men sprint for the brown van. By then the sedan was turning another corner.

Grady didn't slow down once they'd left the van behind. He sped through a light just as it turned red, then rapidly turned three more corners—right, left, right. The maneuver put them on a main boulevard. Justin twisted around in his seat to look out the back window. "I think we've lost them."

Grady relaxed fractionally. He looked back over his shoulder. "Good job, kid. I guess that's another one we owe you."

"Uh, boss." Hacker was looking into his side view mirror. "We've got trouble coming!"

Justin swiveled around again. The brown van had just edged out onto the boulevard about a block behind them.

"Blast it!" Grady slammed his palm against the steering wheel. "These guys are good!" He glanced into his rearview mirror. "Hold on! We're almost there!"

Putting on a burst of speed, he swerved to the right, barely avoiding collision with a sixteen-wheeler. Another swerve placed the sedan into the outer lane of traffic. Just a few yards ahead was a freeway entrance. Justin let out a whoop of triumph as he saw the brown van swept forward into the flow of traffic. "You've got 'em! They're gone!"

"They'll be back," Grady said. Maneuvering onto the freeway, he crossed all six lanes of traffic in one continuous move. Justin's palms showed little half-moons where his nails had dug in, but his hazel eyes glowed with admiration and excitement. This was beginning to look like a high-speed chase in an action movie!

Grady sped down the first off-ramp and turned onto another wide boulevard. Slowing down, he looked back at Justin.

"OK, Justin, here's the plan. Jump out as soon as I stop. Get over to Boeing and get those files. Your father should be out for a couple of hours. I'll call you when I can."

Justin nodded. He slid a hand into his jacket. In all the excitement, he'd actually forgotten what had started all this chase, but the black pouch was still there. He scooted over to the door.

Grady slowed as they came to a major intersection. "Go!"

Justin was out of the car even before it had stopped. Darting to the sidewalk, he ducked behind a parked car. Back where they had turned off the freeway, a brown van was nosing into traffic. Grady was right—the guys in the van *were* good! Missing the freeway on-ramp, they had simply raced on to the next off-ramp, guessing—or hoping—that Grady would take the first exit.

The dark blue sedan peeled off with a squeal of tires. Justin crouched behind the parked car until the van sped by. Straightening up, he stared anxiously after the two speeding vehicles. What if those men caught up to Grady and Hacker?

He pushed the thought out of his mind. Grady was a professional. He could shake those guys! In the meantime, Justin had his own job to do. He broke into a run, not slowing down until he came to a bus stop. A half hour later, he was at the gates of the Boeing research facility.

Justin didn't have the security pass Dad always gave him when he visited his office, and his one worry had been how he was to get past the front gate. But the security guard on duty was one he had met several times before. It was, in fact, the same guard who had been there the day he toured the prototype for the new Boeing airbus.

"Hey, Charlie!" Justin called up. "Is my dad still here? You know, Ron Parker? Can I get through to his office?"

"Hi, Justin." The guard cracked open the window of the guard box. "I'm afraid you missed your dad. He left almost an hour ago."

"Great!" Justin's exclamation brought a strange look from the guard, and he added hurriedly, "I don't want my dad to know I'm here. It's a surprise."

"Oh?" Charlie gave Justin a broad wink. "Someone's birthday coming up, I'll bet."

The gate creaked open. "Make it quick!" he called down. "You really shouldn't be in here without a security pass."

Justin nodded and hurried through the gate.

"Hey, Justin, wait!" Charlie called him back with a frantic wave of the hand. Justin skidded to an impatient stop, but his eyes brightened when he saw the small, plastic tag the security guard was holding out to him.

"So no one'll give you any hassle," Charlie told him with a grin. "Just don't let them get a look at my ugly mug on the front."

Justin clipped the security pass to the front of his jacket. Waving his thanks, he broke into a run. If his father had been gone almost an hour, he might not have much time left!

The security guard in the front lobby was the usual day guard Justin had seen every time he visited his father's office. Stopping a few feet away Justin called out a greeting and tapped his security pass. The guard waved him on by. Before he walked to his father's office, Justin leaned over the counter and hissed, "Hey, Mr. Wu! If my dad comes, please don't tell him I'm here. It's a surprise!"

With a grunt of consent, the security guard went back to his surveillance monitors. Justin headed for the research wing. He passed several lab technicians in white coats on the way, but none cast more than a casual glance at his security badge. This was even easier than he'd hoped.

His father's office was halfway down a long corridor of identical doors. He knocked. A cheerful voice called, "Come in."

Dad's secretary looked up from her desk as Justin stepped into the room. She was a plump, middle-aged woman with a pleasant face and glasses that were continually sliding down her nose. "Why, Justin! What are *you* doing here?"

"Hi, Miss Pettigrew. Is my dad in?" Justin stole a quick glance around the office.

"No, I'm afraid Mr. Parker was called out unexpectedly." Miss Pettigrew's plucked eyebrows arched high. "He didn't say you'd be in this morning, Justin. Aren't you supposed to be in school?"

"He didn't know I was coming," Justin admitted. Remembering the first guard's assumption, he added with a conspiratorial whisper, "It's a surprise. You know—that special day coming up."

He didn't dare elaborate as his dad's secretary knew every birthday and anniversary in the family. But Miss Pettigrew was not by nature an inquisitive person. She glanced back at her computer screen with a touch of impatience.

Justin leaned over her desk. "Did Dad say where he was going? And when he'll be back?"

Miss Pettigrew let out a quiet sigh. Pushing up her glasses, she brought her attention back to Justin. "He didn't say much of anything. Some man called about an hour ago. An emergency to do with that latest project of his."

So that was how Grady had gotten Dad out of the way! Justin glanced at his watch. Dad would be back as soon as he found out Grady's "emergency" didn't really exist. He'd have to hurry. He crossed quickly to the door behind Miss Pettigrew's desk. "I'll wait for him in his office."

"Good idea," Miss Pettigrew said crisply, but she smiled at him as she turned back to her computer screen.

Shutting the office door behind him, Justin crossed the thick carpeting to his father's desk. He slid into the office chair. Pulling out the black pouch Grady had given him, he turned his attention to the computer terminal in front of him.

Then, consulting Hacker's instructions, he typed the first of a series of words and numbers. The sequence made no sense to him, but he obeyed all instructions until heavy, red letters spelled *MENU* in the middle of the screen. Below was a short, numbered list. Justin ran down the list until he reached the words *Government Projects.* Justin clicked the mouse until the screen filled with a much longer list of computer files.

The words *CLASSIFIED. PASSWORD ACCESS REQUIRED* blinked ominously at the top of the computer screen. But the list of files below gave no hint of their top secret contents. Instead of some exotic code name, each file was indicated only by the letters GP followed by a number. Consulting Hacker's list of instructions again, Justin moved the mouse to *GP145* and clicked once. The list disappeared. The instruction *Type password* appeared at the top of the screen.

Justin wiped his sweaty hands on his jeans. Now was the test of his boast to Grady. But he knew the last event of any importance in the Parker household: Mom's birthday and the unveiling of the new office just one month before on Wednesday, October 16.

He calculated rapidly in his head. Reducing the date to numbers, he reversed their order, and multiplied the number by 7 and then 6 for Dad's birth month of June. Then he carefully typed *256242* and reached a forefinger for the Enter key.

But his finger hesitated just above the key. He stared at the small row of numbers on the screen. *You can just erase those numbers, push the exit key, and walk out of this office,* a small voice told him. *Just tell Grady you couldn't do it.*

Justin gave a quick shake of his head. It was too late now to back out. Setting his jaw with determination, he stabbed his finger at the Enter key.

For an instant he thought he must have hit the wrong key. Instead of filling up with the figures and diagrams Hacker had told him to expect, the screen went blank—just as it had at Grady's apartment. A warning beep clamored that something was wrong.

Justin stared with numb disbelief. Across the screen blazed the words: *IMPROPER PASSWORD. ACCESS DENIED.*

Chapter Ten

STOLEN

Justin stared in frozen panic at the message on the computer screen. What was he going to do now?

As the warning beep continued to announce his error, he forced himself to move. Frantically he typed in one date after another—his own birthday, his father's, his parents' anniversary—his fingers fumbling as he calculated the numbers. But after each entry, the screen blinked once more: *IMPROPER PASSWORD. ACCESS DENIED.*

Dropping his head into his hands, Justin tried to think. But the warning beep distracted him. Miss Pettigrew must have heard it by now. She'd be in any moment to check out the signal. Or—maybe that beep had already notified the security system that someone was breaking into a classified file!

He tightened his fingers on his short-cropped curls until it hurt. What other happenings of importance had there been lately in the Parker household? The start of school? Or—Justin sat up with sudden excitement. October 19—three days after his mother's birthday! That was the day the twins had helped Danny Nguyen bring about the arrest of the Dragon Tong, the Vietnamese gang that had terrorized the Nguyen family. Had that really been only a month ago?

A tap at the door brought Justin back to the present. Rapidly typing in the numbers *382242,* he stabbed at the Enter key. The warning beep cut off immediately. Dropping his hands into his lap, he swiveled the chair around. When Miss Pettigrew thrust her head around the edge of the door, he was studying the spectacular view of the Seattle skyline through the plate-glass window behind his father's desk.

"Everything okay in here?"

Justin looked up, an innocent expression on his freckled face. Miss Pettigrew wrinkled her forehead. "I was sure I heard a computer beeping!"

"Everything's fine here," Justin reassured her, but his hands were clenched in his lap. He put on a teasing grin. "Probably just your ears ringing. Overwork, you know. I'll tell Dad you need a day off!"

Miss Pettigrew ignored his attempt at humor. "Hmm. Must have been next door," she muttered with a distracted frown.

She closed the door. The computer screen was now filled with unintelligible figures and diagrams. Consulting Hacker's instructions, he picked up the black pouch and took out the silver CD-R. He was about to insert it when he hesitated. Maybe he'd better make sure he was doing this right before making that all-important copy for Grady!

Justin knew where Dad kept a box of recordable compact discs. He'd borrowed one the last time he'd been in the office to copy off computer-generated pictures of the new Boeing airbus, regular 3½" discs lacking the memory for graphic files of that size. Digging into the bottom desk drawer, he pulled out a fresh disc. Dad's CDs were a silvery-blue on one side, which would keep the extra disc from getting mixed with Grady's.

Inserting the disc into the CD drive, Justin began typing in the copy commands. Moments later the screen announced *Files copied*. Satisfied, Justin removed the CD, inserted Grady's silver one and repeated the process. When the screen read *Files copied,* he took out the silver disc and slid the gold one into the CD drive.

The gold CD was running smoothly. Justin leaned back in the office chair to wait. When the screen read *Program finished,* he exited the GP145 project file. Taking out the gold disc, he shoved the instructions and CD-Rs into the black pouch.

He glanced at his watch. The whole process had taken less than ten minutes. He carefully positioned his father's swivel chair exactly as he had found it. Then he left the office.

He stopped at Miss Pettigrew's desk on the way out. "I can't wait any longer. But please don't tell him I was here. It would spoil the surprise."

Miss Pettigrew glanced up from her computer terminal. She gave Justin a suspicious look.

"Oh, get out of here, Justin." Miss Pettigrew tried to look annoyed. "You're holding up my work."

Satisfied that his father's secretary would keep his secret, Justin took off at a run down the corridor. He bounded down the stairs two and three steps at a time. He'd succeeded after all! The precious copy of the invisibility shield plans was now safe in his hands.

"That surprise must have been a hit," Charlie said, as Justin handed back the security pass.

Justin gave the guard a thumbs-up gesture. "Thanks!"

He headed for the bus stop. *Now where? Home or back to school?* It wasn't much of a choice. Mom would be at home now. But if Justin showed up at school, he was likely to be faced with some awkward questions.

A bus pulling up made up his mind for him. This line went nowhere near the junior high but would leave him only blocks from his home. He'd have to hang around outside until Jenny got home from school. But that was better than a run-in with an annoyed teacher.

As he'd expected, his mother's car was in the driveway when he got home. Justin spent the next several hours sitting under the huge, spreading oak tree across the street.

He pulled his jacket closer. A stiff November wind had risen, its dampness bringing with it a threat of rain. It had been a long time since breakfast, and he was getting colder and more ravenous by the minute. If this was how secret agents spent their days, then maybe he wouldn't take Grady up on his job offer after all.

Brushing the wet leaves from a protruding root, Justin leaned back against the massive trunk of the tree. At least it would soon be all over. Wouldn't Jenny's mouth drop open when Abdul's gang was finally arrested? Everyone would know then that Justin had saved them.

"So! You're back!"

Justin sprang to his feet so fast he banged his head on a low branch. "Ouch!" Rubbing the top of his head, he looked across at his sister. "Oh, hi, Jenny."

Jenny was standing just beyond the shelter of the oak tree,

her arms full of books and a backpack over each shoulder. She gave him a long, cool look. "So how did everything go this morning?"

"Just great!" Justin answered hastily. "Everything went fine!" He hurried over to lift his backpack from Jenny's shoulder. "How was school?"

"Okay. The teachers think you're sick." Jenny handed him a sheaf of papers. "I brought home all your assignments."

Shifting her remaining load to a more comfortable position, she started toward the house. "You'd better come on if you want Mom to think we were together."

"Uh, thanks a lot." Swinging his backpack to his shoulder, Justin followed his sister. He had braced himself for Jenny's questions, and her lack of curiosity faintly alarmed him. But this wasn't the time to worry about it. He just hoped Grady hadn't called his house yet! He broke into a run.

"Any calls for me?" was his first anxious demand as he burst in the kitchen door.

Mom arched her eyebrows in surprise. "You don't usually get calls during school hours."

Justin relaxed. Of course Grady would have realized that Justin couldn't come home until after school. His stomach growled as he smelled the fresh batch of chocolate-chip cookies. Dropping his backpack on the table, he reached for a handful.

He was reaching for a second when he heard a familiar engine turn into the driveway. What was Dad doing back this early?

A car door slammed, then quick steps sounded in the gravel driveway. A moment later, Dad's tall figure appeared at the back door. Jenny gave him a cheerful wave. "Hi, Dad. How was work?"

But Dad didn't answer with his usual lighthearted greeting. Quietly shutting the back door, he stepped into the full sunlight of the kitchen window. Justin stiffened. He'd never seen that look on his father's face, and it frightened him!

Dad let his briefcase fall to the floor. Slumping into a kitchen chair, he dropped his head into his hands. Mom asked anxiously, "What is it, honey? Has something gone wrong with your project?"

Justin edged closer to his father. "Did someone steal it?"

Dad raised his head. His lean face looked gray. "Worse!" he said wearily. "It's been completely destroyed! Months of work—years of research—totally wiped out!"

Justin dropped his cookie uneaten on the counter. So it had finally happened—just like Grady had told him to expect. Abdul and his pals had stolen the GP145 and destroyed the files.

"But . . . but how could someone destroy an entire project?" Mom's dark eyes showed her concern and bewilderment. "All those guards, the security precautions!"

Dad reached over and took one of her hands. "It was a virus."

A virus! Dad's words made perfect, horrible sense to Justin. A computer virus was a program designed—often by malicious pranksters—to be entered onto a computer hard drive. There it would destroy all or selected files in the computer's memory. If detected, a virus could be eliminated. But if a contaminated program was used without being checked, the virus could ruin the hard drive.

Dad wearily ran his fingers through his hair. "Someone has managed to design a virus that destroyed not just the computer file with our finished project plans, but every reference in the mainframe to this particular project. Months of work, years of research and data files, have been erased."

"But . . . that would take a genius!" Justin exclaimed.

"It would certainly take an expert," Dad agreed. "What's more, an expert who knows an awful lot about the Boeing computer systems and the classified work going on there."

He went on, "The first thing they did was to seal off the main computer banks and send everyone home. I have a feeling they're looking for an inside man—someone with access to the computer banks. You see, we had a phone block on the entire computer system. It would take someone inside the research facility—someone with very high clearance—to insert that virus program."

Someone like Dad! Justin's stomach turned. No wonder the NSA had suspected his father.

A sudden thought lightened his worries. Whoever would be meeting Abdul that night to hand over the GP145, it wouldn't be his father. Justin still didn't understand how Abdul could have conned Dad into passing over classified information on computer CDs. But Dad's present dismay made it clear that he knew nothing about the theft and destruction of the invisibility shield.

No, Abdul definitely had some other accomplice inside Boeing. Someone with the same computer skills as Dad. And when those stolen plans were handed over to Abdul tonight, Grady would be there to retrieve them.

Justin's spirits lifted at the thought of the sandy-haired NSA agent. So far Grady had been one step ahead of Abdul and his terrorist pals all the way. Abdul thought he'd destroyed the

GP145 project. But thanks to Grady, the plans for the invisibility shield were sitting safe and sound under Justin's jacket. And when Grady stepped in tonight to arrest Abdul and his associate, Dad's innocence would be proven once and for all.

Justin shifted his feet restlessly. But where was Grady O'Brian? Was he keeping his own investigation under cover until he arrested Abdul that night? If only he'd call! The sooner those precious CDs were out of his own hands, the better.

The feeling of someone's eyes on him made Justin glance up. His sister was watching him, an odd expression on her face. She looked quickly away. Moving to her father's side, she gave him a tight hug. "Please don't be so sad, Daddy. I'm sure they won't think you had anything to do with it."

Dad hugged her back, but he shook his head. "That's where you're wrong, Jenny. I'm afraid everyone on that program who can handle a computer keyboard will be considered a possible suspect—including me."

He managed a wry smile. "But that's the least of my worries. That project was of vital importance to our nation's security. Not only has it been destroyed, but it seems likely our computer expert stole a copy of the plans before he inserted that virus. In the wrong hands, those plans could mean grave danger for our country."

Justin caught the worry in his eyes. If only he could reassure his father that everything would be all right—that the invisibility shield plans were safe, and in just a few hours, the thief who had stolen them would be in custody!

And why not? Dad wouldn't be seeing Abdul again before it was all over. There was nothing he could give away to the enemy now.

The front doorbell jangled. Mom hurried toward the living room. Justin turned to his father. "Dad . . ."

"Ron!" It was Mom. "There's someone here who wants to speak to you."

Justin shut his mouth with a snap. He *would* get interrupted every time he tried to talk to his father. Dad was already on his feet.

Justin started after him, but now his sister was calling him back. Reluctantly he slumped into a chair. "Yeah?" he growled. "What do you want?"

"I want to know what's going on!" Jenny gave him a cool look. "This project that got wrecked. That wouldn't happen to be the one you and Dad were talking about the other night, would it? Maybe this all has something to do with your little adventure this morning?"

But Justin's sharp ears had just caught the squeak of the front door swinging wide and the sound of footsteps entering the living room. "Shh!" He cut his sister off with a sharp wave of the hand. "Listen!"

Dad had left the kitchen door standing open just a few inches. Now both twins could hear a curt voice demanding, "Ron Parker? Dan Ramirez, National Security Agency."

The *National Security Agency!* So Grady's investigation had at last come out into the open. Grady must have sent one of his agents to pick up the CDs.

Justin jumped to his feet, but Jenny beat him to the kitchen door. Justin tried in vain to see over her shoulder. There was a low murmur of his parent's voices. Then he heard the curt voice again. "You have two choices, Mr. Parker. You can answer my questions right here, or you can come with us."

Justin knit his eyebrows together. *This didn't sound right. What was Grady up to?*

Jenny pulled her head back, her brown eyes wide. "It's the police or something. They're arresting Dad!"

But Justin was already pushing past her to peer around the kitchen door. Two men stood in the living room. Justin had no problem recognizing one of them. The man flashing a badge at his father was the driver of the brown van!

Chapter Eleven

HALTED HANDOFF

Abdul's men are here! And pretending to be NSA agents! Justin edged the door open a little farther. *But why?*

Dad was already leading the two men across the living room. "Of course, I'll answer any questions you have," he told the van driver with a friendly nod. "Have you found out yet how the files were stolen?"

"We have a pretty good idea, yes." There was no answering friendliness in the other man's face. "May I sit down?"

Justin ducked back inside the kitchen. Somehow, he had to warn Dad! He didn't dare let the phony agents see him, but if he could call his father out of the room . . .

He bumped into Jenny who was peering over his shoulder. Of course! He could send his sister into the living room.

"Jenny, could you . . . ?"

But now it was Jenny who was waving Justin to silence. An angry exclamation brought them both crowding back to the door. Dad was on his feet.

"What do you mean, you traced unauthorized copies to my office? That's impossible! I wasn't even in the office this morning. And I assure you my secretary doesn't have access to my password."

"Sit down, Mr. Parker," the van driver ordered sternly. "We have proof."

The twins exchanged a dismayed glance as Dad sank back down to the sofa. Justin's head was spinning.

"They think Dad's the one who wrecked that project," Jenny hissed in his ear. "But that's crazy! There's no way anyone could get . . ."

She stared at her brother, a suspicion dawning in her eyes. Justin felt a guilty flush creep up his neck. "Justin," she whispered. "Where *were* you this morning?"

The shrill ring of the phone saved him. Justin motioned frantically for Jenny to answer it. He had to think! The traitor would have covered his tracks well. But any check of the computer log would be enough to turn up Justin's own intrusion into the mainframe computer. And Abdul's accomplice in Boeing must have tipped him off to that fact!

That's why those guys are here! Abdul knows someone else has a copy of the GP145, and he wants it!

"It's for you, Justin." Jenny waved the receiver. "Come on, Justin," she repeated impatiently. "It's some man. He says it's important."

Grady! He started for the hall. "I'll get it. Just a minute."

Justin ran to his parents' bedroom and grabbed the phone beside the king-sized waterbed. "Grady, they're here!" he hissed.

"Who's there?" The sharp concern in Grady's voice was all Justin could have hoped for.

"Those guys who were after you!" he explained. "Abdul's men! And they're pretending to be NSA agents!"

There was a silence on the other end of the line. Then Grady said, "I was afraid something like this might happen when they spotted you this morning. So, were you able to get the copy?"

"Sure, but now they know I've got it. At least, they think my dad does. They haven't seen me yet." Justin lowered his voice to a whisper. "Grady, I'm scared! Can't you come and arrest these guys?"

Grady's voice came calm and soothing over the line. "The problem is, I'm clear across the Puget Sound—a two-hour drive. I'll do what I can. But get yourself and those CDs away from that house. *Now* before anyone sees you!"

Justin hesitated. He knew the vital importance of keeping the last remaining copy of the invisibility shield out of Abdul's hands. But how could he abandon his family to possible danger? If only he'd had a chance to warn Dad! "But . . . my family . . . those men!"

"Justin, if anyone is in danger here, it's you!" Grady said crisply. "I can assure you that once you—and those CDs—are gone, those men will have no further interest in your family. The best thing you can do for them is get out of there at once!"

When Justin still hesitated, Grady sighed. "Look, Justin. There's a lot more at stake here than you or me—or your family. You've got to keep those CDs out of Abdul's hands. Now, I'm sending a couple of my agents over there to pick up Abdul's men. Your family will be safe enough until they arrive. In the meantime, get out of there—now!"

Grady was right, as usual. And Justin had to admit that he, too, was more than anxious to get those CDs out of the house and into the government agent's hands. "Okay, I'll leave right now. But where do I go? Your apartment?"

"Not the apartment! It's being watched." There was a long pause on the line. Justin could make out a faint murmur of voices as though Grady was consulting with someone. He had to bite his lip to keep back his impatience. Then Grady was back on the line. "Can you make it down to the waterfront?"

"Yeah, I can take the bus, but . . ."

"Good. Meet me on the ferry wharf in one hour. If I'm not there, don't hang around waiting. Abdul may have someone watching. Just take the first ferry across Puget Sound to Bremerton. If I can't make it across, I'll meet you on this side."

With a click, Grady was gone. Justin hung up the receiver. Fortunately so much had happened since he'd gotten home that he hadn't even had time to take off his jacket. The black pouch Hacker had given him was still tucked inside, and he had his bus pass and enough money for the ferry, if necessary.

He slipped back into the kitchen. Jenny wasn't there. Good. That would save an explanation.

Then he heard a cool voice say, "You have a son, I understand. About thirteen or fourteen years old, with red hair?"

Justin's blood ran cold. The driver of the van was asking for him. Scrambling for the back door, he paused only long enough to pull it shut silently behind him. Ducking around the side of the garage, he made his way along a hedge and around the back of the next-door house, then stretched his legs in a sprint for the bus stop.

A bus was pulling up when he got there. Threading his way to the back, Justin kept an anxious watch out the rear window. But he saw no sign of the brown van. After ten minutes, he got off and boarded another bus that would take him straight to the Seattle waterfront. Dropping into an empty seat, he leaned back and took a deep breath. The bus wouldn't reach the waterfront for another forty minutes. Now at last he could relax.

But Justin's thoughts were far from pleasant as he stared out across six lanes of freeway traffic. Things had gotten so complicated.

I'm glad I made those copies, he told himself stoutly. *If I hadn't, Dad's project would be gone for good.*

But he couldn't stop the fears that churned in his mind. Had Grady told anyone that he'd had Justin break into the Boeing computer? That program he'd inserted for Hacker was supposed to trace the real traitor, but that could take time.

In the meantime, if Abdul and his men had so quickly assumed that Dad had made that unauthorized copy of the GP145 files, then the investigative team must have come to the same conclusion. Instead of clearing his father's name, he'd gotten him into even more trouble.

Justin pressed the back of his hands against his eyes. Grady knew that Dad hadn't made that unauthorized copy. But until Grady informed his superiors that *he* was the one responsible, no one would believe that Dad was innocent.

Justin's head ached badly by the time he got off the bus not far from the ferry docks. The sky was overcast, and a chill sea breeze bit through his clothes. He pulled his jacket tight, his nostrils flaring at the sharp tang of salt. But the fresh air blew away his headache, and suddenly the answer to his dilemma was clear.

With a lighter heart, Justin trotted along the waterfront. He stopped at Ye Olde Curiosity Shop long enough to buy a small manila envelope and a dollar's worth of postage stamps. Pulling out the black pouch, he checked the CD-Rs inside. They sure didn't look worth all the fuss being made over them.

"Would you have a scrap of paper and a pen I could borrow?" he asked the clerk. "I need to write my parents."

"Sure." The clerk set a paper and pen on the counter. Justin scribbled a quick letter to his parents. He hadn't dared risk a note earlier, not with those phony NSA agents in the house. But if something should go wrong, he wanted them to know where he was going—and why!

"Great! Thanks a million!" Justin broke into a run, pausing only long enough to thrust the envelope through the slot of the nearest mailbox.

He checked his watch as he skidded to a stop in front of the ferry terminal. It was five o'clock, exactly an hour since Grady's call.

Shielding his eyes against the setting sun, Justin looked around. He saw no sign of the government agent, but a ferry was approaching the pier, its blunt prow churning the choppy waves into a white froth. Maybe Grady was on that boat.

Justin made his way into the terminal. It was even more crowded than the wharf as lines of commuters jostled to buy tickets for the next ferry. He was standing on tiptoe to scan the crowd when he stopped short.

Only a few feet away two Arab men argued in low, passionate voices.

One of the Arabs turned in Justin's direction. His dark eyes narrowed and he muttered a quick phrase to his companion. Justin ducked into the crowd as the other Arab turned to stare in his direction. His thoughts flew to the two Middle Eastern tourists he'd seen on his last visit to the ferry wharf. *Could these be the same guys? If so, they must be Abdul's men! Grady had said someone might be watching.*

But the two men made no move to follow him. A blare of sound overhead announced that the incoming ferry was disembarking. Justin trotted across the terminal to watch the foot passengers crowd their way through the big double doors. When the last passenger had pushed past him without a sign of Grady, he hurried to buy a ticket. There was nothing more to do but obey Grady's instructions and take the ferry back across the Puget Sound to Bremerton.

Justin leaned his elbows on the metal rail of the ship. The sun had disappeared behind the far shoreline, and the water looked gray and cold. The waves were choppy and crested with foam, rougher than he'd ever seen them.

Overhead, a seagull gave his wild, lonely cry. Sudden tears pricked at Justin's eyes. Never had he felt so alone. Jenny, at least, had always been at his side on every other adventure. As the twilight darkened to night, he stared out across the water with unseeing eyes. *What if Grady isn't on the other side either? What then?*

Quick footsteps echoed across the metal deck. "Justin?"

Justin spun around. "Grady! Where were you? I thought I'd missed you!"

The government agent clapped Justin on the shoulder. "I saw you looking for me, but I decided to wait for you to board the ferry." He held out his hand. "You got the CDs?"

Justin nodded, sliding one hand into the front of his jacket.

The sight of the government agent had lifted his worries. He'd soon be rid of the discs and the whole mess. But there was still one thing he had to do.

Pulling out the black pouch, he unzipped it to show Grady a glimpse of gold and silver. The stocky agent stared down at the pouch, an odd, unreadable expression on his face. He whistled softly. "So you've really done it. I honestly didn't think you could. Good job, Justin!"

He reached for the pouch, but Justin snatched it away. Zipping it back up, he stuffed it inside his jacket. "I'm sorry, Grady. I can't let you have them. Not yet, anyway."

Grady couldn't hide his exasperation. "Just give me the pouch!"

Justin backed along the ferry rail just out of reach. "I can't!"

Taking a deep breath, he launched into the speech he'd been rehearsing. "You asked me to help you catch those terrorists. Well, I've done everything you've asked. Not just to help my father, but . . . well, because of all that stuff about the security of the United States. Now I want you to do something for me. And . . . and I can't give you the CDs until you do it."

"Why you little . . ." Grady took a purposeful step forward, his square features hardening with anger. Justin backed farther away along the rail. For one long moment, the man and the boy locked eyes. Justin's heart pounded, but he met the steel-gray gaze without flinching.

It was Grady who dropped his gaze first. Some of the anger left his face. "Maybe you do deserve something for your help," Grady said with a shrug. "It's not the first time we've had to pay off an informant. So what do you want? A new bike? Cash?"

"Of course not!" Justin's back was stiff with outrage. "I don't want anything for me. I want you to tell those guys who are investigating that you're the one who made me copy those files. And I want you to tell the National Security Agency that my dad's innocent."

"And risk tipping off our traitor at Boeing?" Grady answered sharply. "He still has to turn those plans over to Abdul. I've already told you I'd take care of your father, but can't this wait a few hours?"

"Then I'll hold onto the CDs until you do." Justin's freckled face was stubborn. "I mean, you said you just needed the plans so you could arrest Abdul. Well, I've got 'em, so go ahead and arrest him."

Justin paused to take a breath. To his relief, Grady no longer looked angry. He stumbled on. "You told me even your bosses think my dad's guilty. I can't give you the CDs until I know Dad's out of trouble."

"Then we'll have to take them!"

Justin swung around with a gasp. He groaned inwardly when he caught sight of Hacker leaning against the ship rail.

Hacker sauntered toward Justin, an ugly smile playing around his mouth. Justin ducked behind Grady.

"Stay away from me!" he panted. "Or I'll never give you the CDs!"

"You are having some trouble?"

The question in strongly accented English brought Justin's head around with a jerk. It was the same two Arabs he had seen arguing in the ferry terminal.

Forgetting Hacker and the black pouch, Justin clutched at

Grady's arm. "Grady, those men! I saw them on the wharf. They must have followed me here!"

The two Arabs walked toward them. One of the men carried a large briefcase. Justin drew in a sharp breath as the other man's coat flapped open, exposing a shoulder holster underneath. "Grady, they've got guns! They must be Abdul's men."

But Grady's square features showed only irritation as he turned to face the two newcomers. "What are you doing here?" he snapped. "I told you I'd meet you tonight."

"We have a right to protect our investment," one man said. His English was slow but clear.

"You know these guys?" Justin relaxed his grip on Grady's sleeve. "Then they were with *you* that day in the Curiosity Shop. I was sure they worked for Abdul."

"Abdul?" The second Arab stepped forward, his black eyes hard with suspicion. "Who is this Abdul, Grady O'Brian? Have you sold this—what do you call it—'invisibility shield' to a competitor?"

"Sell?" Justin looked up at Grady, a slow, cold fear rising in his stomach. "What's he talking about?"

Grady ignored the question. Turning, he jerked his head toward Justin. "The boy's got the plans. Do you have the money?"

Justin stared, appalled. His gaze swept from the two Arabs to the government agent.

"Grady, what are you saying?" he whispered. "That *you* stole the invisibility shield? That . . . that there never was a traitor in Boeing?"

"Just you, Justin," Grady answered cheerfully. "And you've been kind enough to deliver the plans right into our hands!"

Chapter Twelve

DOUBLE-CROSSED!

Justin pressed backward, his mind spinning dizzily. This had to be a nightmare!

"Grady!" he pleaded, still in a whisper. "You're joking, right?"

"Oh, it's no joke. These two men are representatives of a Middle Eastern political faction. They've commissioned me to obtain the GP145." Grady was smiling—that same heart-warming grin that had won Justin over from the start. But this time Justin didn't respond.

"You mean, they're terrorists," he said bitterly, stuffing his hands in his pockets to warm them.

His mind was still reeling. How could this man he'd trusted be a traitor?

He shook his head with bewilderment. "I don't get it. You showed me your ID. That badge was from the National Security Agency just like you said. And that stuff about the invisibility shield—about my dad's work—it was all true. If you're not a real agent, how could you know all that?"

"Oh, I was a government agent, all right," Grady said cheerfully. "That is, until a few years back. The credentials were from my Agency days. As for the invisibility shield, an old military contact let me in on that. When I found a buyer, I started working on a plan to get the GP145 file."

"Then you really were going to kidnap my dad!" The conversation Justin had overheard a few days earlier now made sense. "That's why you were following us that day."

"That was our first plan." Grady threw a disgusted look at Hacker. "Thanks to this idiot's faulty information, *you* messed up that attempt. Not that I'm complaining. Your little interference was the best piece of luck we've had. Anyway, once we found out your father was no scientist, Hacker here tried to break into the mainframe computer. When that didn't work—well, you know the rest."

Justin *did* know the rest. He felt sick as he realized how completely the renegade agent had tricked him. And if the two Arabs hadn't walked in, he'd have handed over those CDs without ever guessing what Grady really was.

The former agent held out his hand again. "Look, Justin, you've been a great help, and I really don't want to hurt you. How about we end this so everyone's a winner. Just give me the pouch, and we'll all walk away. You'll have your life back—and so will your family. Okay?"

The smile in his gray eyes was so warm and compelling that for one instant Justin found himself starting to reach into his jacket. Then a sudden, horrible picture—a picture of invisible missiles and fighter planes launched against an unsuspecting United States—broke the spell of that friendly voice. As if he'd trade his country to save his own skin, even if he believed for a second these men would let him walk out of here to warn the police!

Justin glanced around desperately. There had to be someone on this crowded ferry who could help him! But the other passengers were all up on the observation decks, and the four men who surrounded him blocked any dash for freedom.

Folding his arms across his jacket, he glared his defiance at Grady. "I'll never give you these CDs! Touch me and I'll scream!"

But Grady only laughed. "Go ahead and scream. If someone comes, they're not going to be too happy about being dragged down here by some disobedient kid who's run off with his dad's office documents. And with three witnesses, I don't think anyone's going to believe you're not really my son."

Justin hesitated. Would any passerby believe his accusations of spies and international plots against the word of all these adults? Even to him, the story sounded incredible.

Grady was still smiling. "So you see, Justin, you really *will* have to hand over those CDs. The Islamic Front for World Liberation isn't known for its patience."

He gave a nod, and Hacker and the two others closed in on Justin. Before they could grab him, Justin snatched the black pouch from inside his jacket. Holding it over the rail, he said hoarsely, "Get back! I'll drop it if you don't!"

With a sharp hand gesture, Grady ordered the three men back. They obeyed, scowling and muttering angrily to each other. Hacker only sneered, "He's bluffing! That's the last copy of his dad's project. He wouldn't destroy it."

"I'm not bluffing!" Justin's voice rose shrill and loud despite his efforts to seem calm. "I'd rather no one had the invisibility shield than you guys."

"No, he's not bluffing," Grady said shortly, watching Justin with narrowed eyes. He motioned Hacker back.

"This is ridiculous," Hacker snarled, obeying with obvious reluctance. His thin hands were clenching and unclenching at his sides.

But Grady was looking more amused than angry. "OK, Justin, I guess we're at a stalemate. You're not going to give us those CDs, and we're not about to walk away and leave you with them."

He leaned back against a nearby car. "I think you'll get tired of holding that pouch out there before we get tired of waiting."

With dismay, Justin realized that Grady was right. Already, his arm ached from holding the pouch out over the boiling froth of the ferry wake. He threw a frantic glance over his shoulder. It was night now, but directly ahead he could make out Deer Island looming almost invisibly against the blackness of the overcast sky. A few distant lights clearly marked the ranger station and ferry dock.

Justin glanced again at the growing bulk of the island. The ferry soon would be docking to pick up the last of the day's sightseers, and he knew Grady's threat of claiming him as his son was not idle. If he didn't make a move in the next few minutes, any chance of keeping the CD-Rs out of the terrorists' hands would be lost. Dropping his eyes to the churning foam that bubbled up ghostly white around the bow of the ferry, he had a sudden desperate idea. If he could just keep Grady talking!

"Uh . . . Grady? There's still one thing I don't get. If you're working for these guys, then who's Abdul? Were you trying to sell him the invisibility shield, too?"

"Abdul! Again, this Abdul!" The Arab with the briefcase took a threatening step toward Grady, his eyes flashing. "Who is this man? You promised to deal with no other buyer."

"I haven't the slightest idea who this Abdul is." Grady looked annoyed as the terrorist muttered an angry phrase in Arabic to his partner. "Just some foreigner I saw talking to Ron Parker. He's probably some Third World diplomat begging for technical assistance from Boeing."

"What? You mean, Abdul isn't a spy at all?" Justin almost dropped the pouch. "But . . . you knew all about him. You told me his name."

"*You* told me his name," Grady said softly as he broke off. "You were so sure that Arab looked like a terrorist—a piece of luck that made it a lot easier to get your help!"

Red crept up Justin's neck, but he went on doggedly. "Then those guys at my house—the brown van that was following us— they're not Abdul's men? They really are from the National Security Agency?"

Grady grinned. "My old Agency buddies. Something must have tipped them off that I was going after the invisibility shield. That's one more thing I owe you, Justin. They'd have had me this morning at the apartment if you hadn't tipped me off."

"I wish I'd let them catch you," Justin muttered. A quick glance told him that the dark outline of Deer Island was now much closer, and he added hurriedly. "But . . . the virus! If there wasn't any real spy in Boeing, then who destroyed those files? My dad said it took a real computer whiz to put that virus together."

A mocking laugh exploded from the shadows to his left. Justin twisted to stare at Hacker, who was lounging against the rail, a contemptuous sneer on his thin lips. "You! You made that virus! But how could you get it into the computers? You'd have had to be inside the research facility."

Then a horrible realization squeezed at his stomach. "Oh, no," he whispered. "*I* did it, didn't I? That gold CD. If there wasn't any traitor, then that program had to be . . ."

Justin could no longer contain his anger. "You used *me* to ruin my dad's whole project!" he exploded.

Hacker's sneer slipped for an instant under Justin's outraged glare. Turning his back, he demanded angrily. "Are we going to put up with this all night, Grady? Just grab the kid and get those CDs!"

But Grady cut him off with a sharp motion of his hand. Still grumbling, Hacker subsided and Justin took a deep breath. He thought he'd felt the ferry begin to slow. If only the others hadn't noticed!

Thrusting his arm further over the rail, he turned back to Grady. "So why'd you do it, Grady? How could you betray your country after all that talk about national security?"

Grady gave a short, humorless laugh. "The only security I care about now is my own. Oh, yes, I'm in it for the money. That briefcase over there has a few million dollars in it that's going to keep me comfortable for the rest of my life."

He straightened up from the side of the car. "Come on, Justin. Am I really such a bad guy? I haven't let these guys hurt you, have I? And I wouldn't worry so much about national security. By the time the Arab Front for World Liberation ever figures out how to use the invisibility shield, I'm sure your father and his friends will have found a way to neutralize it. Look, I'll even share with you—say fifty-thousand dollars?"

A flicker of movement from the corner of his eye brought Justin's head up with a jerk. He caught his breath in alarm. While Grady had held his attention, Hacker and the Arabs had been circling around to close in on him. The one-time government agent had fooled him again!

Making a desperate lunge for the pillar that supported the deck above, Justin hauled himself onto the rail, keeping the black pouch out over the water. The metal deck rail was slick with salt spray but he managed to pull himself to a standing position. His stomach heaved in rhythm with the ferry as he looked out across the rolling darkness of the Sound.

He swayed. The waves rushed up at him. Through a roaring in his ears, he heard Grady shout, "Get down from there, you fool! Someone get that kid down before he falls!"

Hands grabbed at his ankles. Justin kicked out with all his strength. Stuffing the pouch back into his jacket, he took one last glance at the white froth below and drew in a deep breath. Then, as hands snatched at him again, he jumped!

Chapter Thirteen

FROZEN WATERS

The water closed over Justin's head, the shock of its winter chill driving the breath from his lungs. The frothing bubbles tore at him, tumbling him over and over as though he were caught in a giant's washing machine. He kicked upward, snorting as the salt water stung his nostrils. But he hadn't reckoned with the sheer force of the water churned by the passing ferry.

It's pulling me under the boat! Justin struck out frantically, suddenly panic-stricken as he fought the pressure that pushed him deep below the surface of the water. His lungs burned with his need for air. Then, just as he knew he would have to inhale—even if it meant his lungs filling with seawater—a last, desperate kick carried him beyond the turbulence of the ferry wake.

Breaking the surface of the water, he gasped in a long, shuddering breath. The ferry was still sliding past him only a few yards to his right. Justin could make out several dark forms silhouetted against the deck lights. They were running along the edge of the car deck toward the rear of the ferry.

"I have seen him!" The guttural foreign accent rang out over the water. The running figures crowded to the back rail. Then something smacked the water only inches from Justin's head.

As the ferry's circle of light moved away, another smack sprayed his face with salt water.

They're shooting at me! They're using silencers! Reacting at last, Justin dove deep beneath the surface. He stayed under until his lungs were bursting. When he broke the surface again, the ferry was gone. Even the glow of its lights had disappeared beyond the tossing waves.

Just in front of him a wave crested, its tip foaming ghostly white. Curling over, it slapped him full in the face. Justin went under again, sputtering and snorting. He struggled back to the surface, gagging on the seawater that filled his throat. Shaking his head to clear his eyes, he looked around for the black bulk of Deer Island.

It wasn't there! A bitter wind, reaching the Puget Sound from a winter squall far out to sea, lashed the salt water to a frenzy. The heavy swells that had looked so rough from the ferry deck now rose high above Justin's bobbing head.

A slow drizzle pattered against his upturned face. No hint of moon or starlight filtered through the rain-swollen clouds. He was swimming now in a rolling, heaving darkness so black he could barely make out the hand he waved in front of his eyes.

Justin knew that Deer Island lay only a few hundred yards away. But caught in the trough between two long rollers, all he could see was the faint glimmer of the cresting waves. *Where is the island?*

He tried to still his chattering teeth, to think clearly. His plan had seemed so easy from the ferry deck. He would jump into the water when the ferry neared Deer Island. He was a good swimmer and could easily swim a few hundred yards. Once on shore, he could make his way to the ranger station. There it would just be a matter of calling his parents and the police.

But now, unable to see the black outline of the island above the frenzied waves, he didn't even know which way to swim. And already the bitter chill of the seawater bit through his clothes. He couldn't last long in these icy waters!

A surging wave caught him from underneath, tossing him high. He gasped as he glimpsed the warm glow of the Seattle skyline far off to his right, the Space Needle rising against the night sky. To his left was the welcome twinkle of the ranger station, the lighted silhouette of the ferry bobbing at its nearby docks.

Turning his back on the distant outline of the city, Justin began swimming toward those lights. Doggedly he climbed to the top of each heavy swell, then dropped again into a darkness that left him once more disoriented. Only when a larger-than-usual roller lifted him high was he able to make out the silhouette of Deer Island. Then he corrected his course and swam on.

He'd been kicking and struggling for what seemed hours when he realized that the twinkling safety of the ranger station never seemed to draw any closer. In fact, each fresh glimpse of those distant lights seemed to have drifted farther off to his left. He'd been caught in an ocean current! Justin kicked with a new desperate strength. He had to reach the shore before that current swept him past the island!

He'd covered more than half the distance when he realized he might not make it! What would have been an easy swim on a warm summer day was a different matter with winter temperatures only a few degrees above freezing. His arms and legs moved only mechanically now. Some far-off corner of his mind wondered dully if the black pouch was still inside his jacket, but his hands were too frozen to feel for it. His whole body was numb with cold and exhaustion. Each time a wave crashed over his head, it took longer to struggle back to the surface.

Slowly the water seemed to turn warm. The burning chill left his limbs. In fact, he no longer felt much of anything except an overwhelming desire to sleep. He stopped swimming. If he could just float here a few minutes. Maybe close his eyes for a short rest.

Hypothermia! A slow realization of danger crept into his sluggish brain. The sleepiness and false sense of warmth were the signals of a dangerously low body temperature. He *had* to get out of these icy waters—and fast!

Justin treaded water long enough to kick off his shoes. This was more difficult than he'd expected since he could no longer feel his feet. But the relief of that weight gave him strength to begin swimming again.

A swell rose beneath him, carrying him up, up—farther than he had yet been. The lights of the ranger station were still far to his left, but his numbed mind slowly registered the crash of waves against a rocky shore somewhere ahead. *You're almost there. You've got to keep going!*

His frozen limbs no longer obeyed him. Helplessly, he slid down the other side of the wave. With sleepy fascination, he stared up at the slope of the wave. It was bigger than he'd thought, swollen perhaps by the rising tide and the storm out at sea. And it seemed to be growing, reaching above him in a black, menacing peak!

As Justin watched, the huge mass of salt water curved slowly inward, the foam on its tip reaching a long, ghostly hand down toward him. Only then did some instinct of self-preservation shock his brain awake. *Oh, no! It's breaking and I'm underneath!*

But Justin couldn't force himself to move. Like a slow-motion replay, the breaking wave curled in on itself. For one endless moment, it seemed to hang, the foam-crested tip far above his head.

Then gravity won its battle, and thousands of pounds of seawater crashed down in a boiling, frothing lather. This time, Justin no longer had the strength even to lift his head. As the weight of the water carried him below the surface, something long and ropelike reached up to wrap itself around his ankles.

With dull surprise, he realized, *I'm drowning!*

Chapter Fourteen

MANHUNT

Justin floated facedown. Wave after wave tugged at his body, bumping him slowly forward. Something sharp scratched his cheek. The sudden pain brought him to full consciousness again. It was a long moment before he realized that it was sand and rock that scraped at his body. Something solid lay under his frozen hands.

Somehow Justin struggled to his feet. Pulling away a strand of seaweed that had wrapped itself around his ankles, he staggered through the breakers toward the shore.

There was no real beach, just a steep, rock-strewn bank slanting up to the hiking trail that ran around the island. Justin had been swept far to his left by the current, and the lights of the ranger station were now hidden around the curve of the island. Pushing through the tangle of brush that edged the shore, he sprawled onto the smooth surface of the path.

He knew he couldn't lie there for long. The brush and trees around him cut off the chill sea wind, but it was still not much warmer here than in the water. As feeling crept back into his arms and legs, he began to shiver. He had to get to the warmth and shelter of the ranger station.

Stumbling to his feet, Justin opened his jacket a few inches and felt inside. To his relief, the pouch was still there. Tucking his numbed hands into his armpits, he started down the path in a shambling trot.

A foghorn blared as the path opened onto the park land that sloped to the ranger station. The ferry's twinkling outline was just disappearing around the curve of the island as it headed for the far shore of the Puget Sound.

The last ferry of the day! he thought forlornly, wiping the drizzle from his face with a wet sleeve. *How will I get home?*

But as he started down the grassy slope, he decided it was just as well the ferry had gone on without him. *At least I won't have to worry about running into Grady and his goons.*

At the bottom of the slope, he trotted along the wooden boardwalk that edged the water. The scattered buildings of the ranger station were dark except for the small, wood-framed house where the park ranger lived. The welcoming glow of those windows pulled Justin like a magnet. In a few moments, he'd be warm and safe. He'd call Dad, and this whole nightmare would be at an end.

The porch was lit by one small bulb. Running eagerly up the front steps, Justin raised a fist to hammer on the door.

Grady's cold, angry voice stopped him short. "I told you not to shoot the kid! If we don't get those plans, it's going to cost your necks!"

Justin stood paralyzed with shock, one hand still raised. Then the sound of quick footsteps sent him diving for cover. He ducked behind a rain barrel set under the nearest window just as the front door creaked open. Grady's frowning face peered out into the darkness, then the door slammed shut.

"I thought I heard someone," he heard Grady say. "Maybe it's the boy."

"He never came up after those shots," Hacker's voice snapped. "He probably drowned. A hundred million dollars down the drain."

Raising his head cautiously, Justin peered over the edge of the windowsill. He looked into the park ranger's cozy home. A fire crackled merrily in the stone fireplace. Justin eyed the dancing flames with longing. He was so cold.

But the rest of the scene wasn't as cozy. There were five men in the room. Hacker lounged in an armchair near the fire, a cigarette in his thin fingers. Near the door stood the two Arabs, their guns hanging loosely from their hands. One still carried the briefcase chained to his wrist.

The fifth man was the young park ranger Justin had seen with his parents the first day he'd met Grady. The ranger sat slumped over, blood trickling from a cut over one eye. Grady was winding a length of rope around his wrists and ankles.

I should have known! Justin told himself savagely. Grady and his men must have guessed that he'd head straight for the island.

But now they, too, were stranded. Would they really stay until the first ferry the next day?

Justin soon found out. Giving a last tug to the knots that bound the young park ranger, the renegade secret agent pulled what looked like a small transistor radio from a pocket and tossed it to one of the terrorists. "Let your friends know we'll be a bit late. We've got to search the island for the kid."

"Aw, come on! It's raining out there," Hacker protested. He lit another cigarette from the stub of the last one. "Besides, those

CDs will be worthless after a dunking in seawater. Just call in the yacht and get us out of here."

"I'm not stupid!" Grady retorted coldly. "That pouch I gave the kid was waterproof. If he's made it to the island, then those plans are still good."

They have a yacht out there, Justin realized as the man pulled an antenna to full length and spoke tersely in Arabic. *That's how they're going to get those plans out of the country.*

Ducking away from the window, Justin ran along the side of the house. He was shaking, as much from fear as from cold.

Silently, he slipped around the back. Somehow, he had to keep those discs away from the terrorists. But first he had to get warm! If only he could find an old tarp or rug.

He was trotting through the night toward what looked like a toolshed when he ran right into something furry. Biting back a startled yelp, he ran cautious hands over what had blocked his way. His heart raced with sudden excitement as he recognized the distinct feel of wool beneath his hands. He had stumbled into an old blanket hanging from a clothesline.

Yanking down the blanket, he wrapped it around his shoulders. It was damp and smelled strongly of wood smoke and fish, but Justin didn't care. Now all he needed was a place to hide. And he knew just where to go!

He climbed back up the slope toward the shelter of the woods. A door crashed open behind him. He had reached the entrance to the hiking path when he heard Grady shout, "That blanket's gone! He's here all right. Split up and search both sides of the island."

Justin knew he had to leave the trail, but first he had to find what he was looking for.

There! He'd almost missed it in the dark. The path dipped right down to the shore here, forming a flat, rocky beach where he and Jenny had often dug for shells and ocean-polished rocks when they were small. That funny boulder that always made Jenny think of a squat, fat Santa Claus was still there, a black outline against the faint glimmer of the breakers.

Turning away from the beach, Justin ducked into the bushes on the far side of the path. In a straight line from that squat boulder was their secret hideout—a cave carved into the tangled roots of two ancient trees.

They'll never find me there. If only I can find it! Suddenly a beam of light dazzled his eyes. Instinctively Justin dropped to a crouch. Above his head, the powerful flashlight played back and forth through the woods. A murmur of voices reached his ears from the path that was still only a short distance away.

At last, the light disappeared, and Justin rose to his feet. He bit his lip as he stepped on a sharp twig. Now that his feet were throbbing back to life, he could feel every scrape and bruise.

Ignoring the pain, he pushed farther into the brush. Branches left painful scratches across one cheek, but he didn't dare slow his pace. It wouldn't take long for Grady and his men to search the footpath and shore. He had to find that hiding place soon!

He was beginning to despair when he suddenly stumbled into the open. Stifling a gasp of thankfulness, he peered into the darkness. Yes, this had to be the spot. The hideout should be straight ahead.

He had taken only a few steps across the clearing when he froze. He listened without breathing. Yes, there it was—the deep whoosh of an exhaled breath! Then he heard a faint rustle in the grass. Someone—or something—was in the dark glade with him!

The rustle moved closer. The blood pounded in Justin's ears, and he had to dig his fingernails into the palms of his hands to keep from panicking. *Was one of Grady's men standing nearby in the darkness, waiting for him? Or . . . could it be some wild animal, maybe a bear or a mountain lion?*

Something cool and moist nuzzled softly at his hand. Justin felt a smooth, warm head with two small buds of horn under his fingers. With another soft whoosh, a yearling deer snuffled at his pockets for the food it had come to expect from visitors to the island.

Pushing the deer away, Justin hurried across the clearing until he reached the bushes on the other side. Dropping to his hands and knees, he groped his way until his fingers met a gnarled tangle of protruding tree roots. He'd found the hideout!

But was the den still empty? What if it was now home to some animal—a fox or a wolverine? Justin sat back on his heels, but a shout jerked his head up in alarm. He could see a distant gleam of light probing the woods to his left. He would have to take his chances.

Dropping to his belly, he wormed his way under the brush, then shifted and slid his legs into the hollow.

From inside, Justin tore off a small branch and swept any tracks he'd left outside the thicket. Only then did he slide all the way into the hideout. It was empty. He'd been afraid that the hole would be too small for a husky thirteen-year-old. But once he squeezed through the narrow opening, he found that he could even sit up, his head pressed against the root system that roofed the den.

He began to shiver again. He pulled the blanket tight, tucking the ends under his scratched and bruised feet. His stomach cramped with hunger, reminding him that he hadn't eaten since that chocolate chip cookie he'd snatched from the kitchen. He settled back against the wall of the den. At least he was starting to feel warmer. Dad had once told Justin that wool was the best survival material because it held in body heat even when damp. *Dad was right as usual,* Justin thought drearily.

But even though his body was warming up, a chill of misery and anger sat heavy in Justin's chest. He'd escaped Grady and his men for the moment, but who was he kidding? They had only to wait until daybreak to trace his tracks to this clearing. And unlike his past adventures, he had no hope this time that someone would show up to rescue him. No one—not even Jenny—had the slightest idea where he was.

"Justin! Hey, kid!" The shouts echoed through the woods outside the den. Justin raised his head warily.

"Look, kid! We know you're out there!" Justin stiffened. It was Hacker. A faint glow from the entrance lit the blackness of the den. Hacker was right outside!

The glow of a flashlight beam grew brighter. Someone was approaching his hiding place.

Now, Grady's voice coaxed him. "Look, Justin, you're cold and hungry. You know you can't last out here until morning. Why don't you come on in where it's warm?"

Justin gritted his teeth, stuffing his fists into his ears to shut out that friendly, sympathetic sound. Did Grady really think he'd fall for his lies again?

Justin dropped his hands as the men moved away. He sifted

back through the events of the last weeks. Now that he knew what Grady was, he could see how easily the agent had tricked him into helping him steal the GP145.

One consoling thought lightened his misery. At least Grady's threats of arresting his father had also been a lie. There never had been a traitor on the Boeing research team.

But there was a traitor! Justin sat up, hitting his head on the roof overhead so hard it brought tears to his eyes. *He* was the Boeing traitor! By taking the GP145, he'd endangered the safety of his entire country.

And if Dad *had* been in no danger of arrest, that was no longer true. Not after what Justin had done that morning. Not now that the NSA was convinced Dad had stolen the invisibility shield plans and destroyed years of vital research.

Choking back a sob, Justin dropped his head to his knees. *God, why did you let this happen? It's all your fault! You knew Grady was lying. Why didn't you help me?*

Huddled with his head bowed, Justin realized this was the first time since this nightmare had begun that he had prayed. And as the tears squeezed their way from under his closed eyelids, it was as though a quiet, gentle voice answered, *You never asked me.*

No, he'd never asked God's help in this mess. In spite of the trouble he had thought his father was in, the renegade government agent had made him feel important. Instead of asking God for help, he'd lied—to his parents, to his sister, to his teachers! Then he'd defended his actions by saying that he had no choice. Justin burned with shame.

If I hadn't lied, Dad would have told me Abdul was no spy. He'd have known about Grady in time to keep him from stealing the invisibility shield.

Clenching his fists, Justin prayed silently, *Oh, God, I'm so sorry! I thought I had to lie to help my dad, but I was wrong! Please forgive me and . . . well, I know I don't deserve it, but won't you please help my dad and keep those men from getting his project?*

Nothing had changed inside the cramped den. He was just as hungry, and this hole in the ground was just as damp and crowded, but Justin was suddenly comforted. He wasn't really alone. God was with him, and he had forgiven him.

He felt almost warm now. The exhaustion and emotion of the last hours were catching up with him. His eyes drooped shut. He was almost asleep.

"Justin! Justin, where are you?" The whisper was low and not very far away. "Come on, Justin, are you in there?"

Justin jerked awake as the whispered call was repeated. His eyes strained against the blackness of the den. If it was one of Grady's men out there, he didn't carry a flashlight. But why bother whispering?

"Justin, I know you're there. Come on. Answer me!" The whisper drifted closer. Justin tensed. Someone was searching the brush just outside his hiding place!

Justin didn't breathe. *If he doesn't see anything, maybe he'll go away.*

But already he'd caught the scraping, dragging sound of someone creeping under the brush. Then he heard the patter of falling dirt. A small pebble rolled down the entrance to stop at Justin's feet. His hiding place had been discovered!

Chapter Fifteen

TRAITOR TAKEDOWN

They won't get me that easily! Shifting to a crouch, Justin groped around in the dark. His hand slid across a stone. A soft, hurried breathing told him that his unseen visitor was inching headfirst into the hideout. His heart raced, but he lifted the rock above his head. *When the guy gets close enough, I'll smash his head in!*

His muscles tensed, the rock ready. Then a soft voice hissed, "Justin? It's me, Jenny. Are you in here?"

Justin's mouth dropped open in the darkness. The stone fell from his fingers. He whispered in amazement, "Jenny! How did you get here?"

"I followed you." Sliding forward on her stomach, Jenny pulled herself the rest of the way into the den. The fit was tight, but there was just enough room for her to sit with her legs pulled up to her chest.

Reaching into the darkness, Justin touched a tangle of curls, then brushed his fingers across her face. "Jenny, you're crying. Are you okay?"

"I'm *not* crying!" Jenny whispered crossly. But she sniffed and then muttered, "I thought you'd drowned."

"I almost did." Sliding an arm around her shoulders, Justin gave her a brotherly squeeze. Then he returned with bewilderment to his first question. "I don't get it. How did you know where I was?"

"I was on the other line when you were talking to . . . what did you call him? Oh, yeah, Grady. When he told you to meet him at the ferry wharf with the plans for Dad's invisibility thing, I left and took a bus straight there."

Justin's mouth was still open as she went on. "You never even noticed me following you at the terminal. When that Grady didn't come, I knew you'd have to take the ferry, so I bought a ticket and boarded ahead of you. I was hiding under one of the cars when Grady and those other guys showed up. I was going to get the captain when you jumped over the rail. Then I heard one of the men say he'd shot you."

Jenny's whispered explanation wobbled. She steadied her voice. "I was afraid you'd drowned. But I knew you'd head for the island if you were still alive, so I followed Grady and hid under the wharf until the ferry left. Then I heard them shouting that you had to be here. With all those guys hunting you, I knew you'd head straight for the hideout. So, here I am!"

Justin was amazed. "But . . . how did you know? About Grady and the invisibility shield? I never said anything."

"I'm your twin, Justin," Jenny whispered scornfully. "I knew the minute you started acting so weird that you were mixed up in another of your mysteries. Besides, I recognized that sandy-haired man you were talking to at soccer practice. He was the same guy you said had been following us that day on the wharf."

She added slyly, "The same day you disappeared and came back talking about 'national security'! So I figured the guy must be a government agent. When Dad got so mad about that invisibility thing, I guessed someone must be trying to steal it. I didn't know what you were up to, but I figured you must be helping that sandy-haired guy."

"But how in the world did you know Grady was a traitor?" Justin demanded. He added bitterly, "He sure fooled me."

"I didn't really," Jenny admitted. "Not until I heard you talking with those guys. But I knew something was wrong when you were determined Abdul was a spy. Dad had told me once about Abdul—how he's worked so hard to bring health care and modern technology and all that to his country. *And* how he got shot once by Islamic terrorists who didn't like what he was doing!"

Jenny shifted her legs to a more comfortable position. "Anyway, that didn't sound like a spy to me." She added, "I still don't know why everyone's after Dad's project. When we get out of here, you're going to tell me everything that's happened."

"If we do get out," Justin said sourly. He was impressed at the way Jenny, had pieced everything together, but he felt foolish. He'd been so sure he'd sidetracked his twin.

"Look, Jenny, we're in big trouble! No one knows where we are, and Grady's bound to find us come morning. I wish you'd thought to call Mom and Dad or something."

"Oh, did I leave that out?" Jenny said innocently. Justin could feel her smiling in the dark. "I *did* call—after I untied that park ranger! Dad said they'd be here as soon as Mr. Ramirez—that's the NSA agent that was arresting Dad—could scrape up a helicopter. He said to sit tight until they show up."

Justin was speechless. Finding his voice at last, he said in a fervent whisper, "Jenny, did I ever tell you you're the greatest!"

"Not often enou—" Jenny grabbed her brother's arm. But he'd already heard the voices. Grady and his men were sweeping back through this part of the woods.

"There's no sign of him," Hacker complained just beyond the brush that cloaked the hideout. "Can't this wait until morning?"

"You'll keep searching until he's found!" Grady's voice was unsympathetic. "That is, if you want your share of a hundred million."

The murmur of voices faded. Then, from somewhere across the clearing, Justin heard Grady call, "I'm going to check that ranger. You three split up and search the south end of the island. If you find him, let off a shot."

Jenny whispered, "If Grady finds the ranger loose, he'll know we've called for help!"

Justin nodded. "We've got to warn the ranger!"

Jenny slithered headfirst through the narrow opening of the den. Justin waited for the soft whistle that was their all-clear signal before he followed, reluctantly leaving the wool blanket behind. He shivered as the chill of the winter night bit into his damp clothing.

The bobbing gleam of the searchers' flashlights faded into the distance. Grabbing hands, the two picked their way across the clearing. When they reached the woods, Jenny took the lead, slipping with ghostlike silence from tree to tree.

It didn't take long to reach the hiking trail that led down to the docks. With Grady already ahead of them and the other three men searching the far side of the island, the chance of being seen was small. They'd have to take that chance if they were to reach the park ranger in time. They began to run.

The pair had just reached the backyard of the ranger's house when Justin caught the sound of angry voices inside. As they crept along the side of the house, there was a muffled thud, then a groan.

"The park ranger said he had a shotgun," Jenny whispered hopefully. "Maybe he caught Grady."

Justin shook his head. He didn't think the renegade NSA agent was the sort to be taken unaware by a park ranger. Reaching the window where he had earlier spied on Grady and his men, he peeked in cautiously.

It was just as he'd feared! Grady stood across the living room, the young park ranger sprawled at his feet. With a groan, the ranger rolled over. Pushing himself to his hands and knees, he dove at Grady's legs. But Grady stepped to one side, kicking the ranger in the face. The ranger crashed to the floor.

The renegade agent kicked the groaning park ranger in the ribs. Then, pulling a gun from under his jacket, he leveled the weapon at the ranger's head.

"Who were you calling?" he demanded harshly. "And who cut you free?"

"We've got to help him!" Jenny whispered, her eyes wide with horror.

But Justin had stiffened with sudden excitement. Tapping Jenny on the shoulder, he pointed. Not far from the window, hidden from Grady's view, lay a double-barreled shotgun. A phone dangled by its receiver over the side of a table.

Justin studied the layout of the room. If only they could get that gun! A dark doorway on the far side of the room gave him an idea. "There's got to be a back door," he whispered to Jenny.

"I'll get Grady to come after me. Then you can go in the back and grab that gun."

"No, you get the gun," Jenny whispered back. "You're the one who knows how to use it. I'll distract Grady."

She was right. Jenny disliked guns and had refused to learn to shoot, but Justin protested, "No, it's too dangerous! What if he catches you?"

"There's no time to argue." Jenny started toward the front door, pausing only to hiss. "Hurry up!"

Justin didn't waste any more time. He raced around the back of the house. The back door was unlocked. Easing it open, he stepped inside. The light was off, but the faint gleam of a refrigerator and stove told him he was in the kitchen.

Crossing to the other door, he peered into the living room. Grady still stood in front of the fireplace. The park ranger lay motionless at his feet. Were they too late after all?

Then he heard a loud knock at the front door—Jenny's diversion.

"Who's there?" Grady stepped away from the park ranger, his gun held steady in one hand, barrel pointed toward the ceiling. When no one answered, he started with purposeful strides for the front door.

Good job, Jenny! Now run for it! Dropping to his hands and knees, Justin crawled rapidly across the room. But he had several feet left to go when another impatient pounding rang out. Grady yanked open the door and Justin bit back a cry of dismay as his sister stumbled into the room, her hand still raised for another knock.

Grabbing Jenny by the shoulder, Grady pulled her farther into the room. Slipping his gun into a shoulder holster, he pushed her dark curls away from her face. "You're the Parker girl! Justin's sis—"

Justin saw the realization on the renegade agent's face as he whirled around and reached for his gun. But Justin was already diving for the shotgun. Snatching it up, he leveled it over the back of the armchair.

"Drop the gun, Grady!" he ordered sharply. "Let her go, or I'll shoot!"

Grady pushed Jenny away from him, but he didn't drop the gun. To Justin's horror, the renegade agent began walking slowly toward him, his gun hanging loose in his hand.

"I don't think so, Justin." Grady spoke pleasantly, but his eyes were narrowed and hard. "You're not the type to shoot a man in cold blood."

"But I am!" a grim voice broke in from behind him. "Drop the gun!"

Grady spun around, his features twisted with anger. The park ranger was on his feet. Blood masked one eye, but the small pistol in the other hand was trained rock-steady on Grady. The bottom drawer of a nearby desk stood open.

With a snarl, Grady let his gun slip through his fingers to the floor. Darting forward, Jenny grabbed the weapon and pointed it gingerly at Grady. The park ranger wiped blood from his eyes. With his gun, he motioned toward an armchair. "You! Sit!"

Grady scanned the three guns leveled at him. Then he shrugged and obeyed. The park ranger turned to Justin. "Think you can tie up our friend here? You'll find the rope they used on me in the corner."

"Sure." Justin answered.

He started across the room, the shotgun turned barrel-up in one hand. Without thinking, he passed between the park ranger and their prisoner. In that brief instant, Grady sprang. His heavy body pinned Justin to the ground. Steel-strong hands were tearing the shotgun from his grip.

Bang! An explosion rocked the room. Grady's heavy weight rolled away. Justin scrambled to his feet. The shotgun was still in his hands and hadn't been fired. Gasping for breath, Justin looked across the room. The park ranger had his gun pointed straight at Grady, but he nodded his head toward Jenny. Jenny's face was white as she stared down at the smoking gun in her hand. Her stunned eyes then dropped to the carpet. Justin turned pale as he saw the hole in the carpet just inches from where his head had been.

Hurrying over to Jenny, he carefully lifted the gun from her fingers. "I think I'd better take that."

"And *you* get back in that chair!" the park ranger told Grady. "You try that again, and I'll blow your head off!"

This time Justin was careful not to get between the ranger and Grady. He tied Grady securely to the armchair, using so many knots they would need to cut the rope to get him loose. But as he stepped back to check his handiwork, he noticed a gleam of satisfaction in Grady's cold, steel-gray eyes.

"Something's wrong!" he said tensely. "What are we forgetting?"

"That gunshot!" exclaimed Jenny. "Remember—Grady said to fire a shot if they found you!"

Justin caught the flash of anger on Grady's face. "You're right!

Now they'll think Grady's got me. They might be on their way right now."

The park ranger wiped his hand across his blood-streaked face. "At least two of them have guns. This may be a problem!"

Justin looked around the room, then down at their prisoner. "Maybe not," he said slowly. "I have an idea."

Five minutes later, Justin cast a satisfied glance around the room. Jenny had already slipped into the kitchen. Grady sat facing the fire, his armchair turned at an angle so the ropes wouldn't be visible from the door. Several layers of clear tape provided an invisible gag. The park ranger lay in a huddle at his feet.

Justin had just stepped behind the drapes when he heard running steps outside. A moment later, the door slammed open. Hacker and the two terrorists crowded into the room.

Hacker stopped short when he saw Grady's silhouette. "So you're taking a rest while we're out freezing!" he exclaimed angrily. "Where's the kid?"

"Right here." Justin stepped out from behind the curtains, swinging the shotgun to cover the three men. The park ranger jumped to his feet and ordered, "Get your hands up, or I'll shoot!"

"Don't even think about it!" Jenny moved in from the kitchen. She held Grady's gun steady with both hands. Justin grinned as one of the men hastily dropped his hand away from his jacket. If they only knew that he'd emptied the bullets from her gun!

"Now drop your guns and back up against that wall!" commanded the ranger. The two Arabs tossed their guns to the carpet. The park ranger and Justin kept their weapons pointed at the three men while Jenny carefully picked up the discarded guns and placed them at the ranger's feet.

"Now all we have to do is wait for that helicopter to show up. Won't Dad be surprised!"

Justin was just finishing the last knot on his three new prisoners when an amused voice said, "Anyone here need help?"

"Dad!" Forgetting the men she was helping to guard, Jenny hurled herself across the room. Justin dropped the end of the rope and sighed in relief.

Dad glanced around the room, one eyebrow raised. "Well, it looks like you two have everything under control!"

Only then did Justin notice the two men who had entered the living room behind his father. Mr. Ramirez, the NSA agent who had driven the brown van, crossed the room to look down at Grady, still gagged.

"If it isn't O'Brian!" Mr. Ramirez said. He shook his head as his gaze moved from the renegade agent to the other three prisoners. "Who in the world will ever believe Grady O'Brian was brought down by a couple of kids."

Grady's eyes burned with hatred. Still grinning, Mr. Ramirez strolled over to the three Parkers. Turning to Justin, he said, "I've only got one question right now. *Where are the plans for the GP145?*"

In the last hour, Justin had completely forgotten about the black pouch. Unzipping his wet jacket, he reached inside. "They're safe!" he said proudly. "On these CDs. . . ."

Justin pulled out the pouch and felt a sloshing inside the bag. Turning it over, he stared with horror at the small slit in the zip-lock closure that kept it watertight. Somewhere in all the crashing and scraping in the sea and on the rocks, the black pouch must have torn open.

Grabbing the pouch from Justin's hands, Mr. Ramirez turned it upside down. A stream of water and sand spilled to the floor. The NSA agent pulled out a silver disc. Justin could see the scratches and an ominous crack that ran across it.

"This CD is ruined," the NSA agent said tightly, holding up the dripping disc. "We've lost the GP145 plans for good!"

Chapter Sixteen

THE TRUTH COMES OUT

Dad took the ruined CD-R from Mr. Ramirez and turned it over in his hands. "This is worthless, all right." Dad glanced over at Justin and sighed. Then he placed a hand on his son's shoulder and smiled sadly.

"Don't blame yourself, Justin. It wasn't your fault. And besides, thanks to you, we're rounding up a whole network of spies and international terrorists!"

"But, Dad, I . . ."

"Not now, Justin. . . ." Dad held up his hand as the roar of a motorboat drowned out Justin's attempted explanation. This was followed by heavy boots thudding up the boardwalk from the docks.

The arrivals turned out to be the police reinforcements Mr. Ramirez had requested earlier. The helicopter in which Dad and the NSA agents had arrived was settled onto the grassy meadow where the deer fed just beyond the docks. Justin didn't have another chance to speak with his father until the four prisoners were escorted to the helicopter under the supervision of the other NSA agent. The park ranger, despite strong protests, was also dispatched to the hospital, and Mr. Ramirez assigned a police sergeant to keep watch on the island until the park service could be notified.

When the three Parkers were alone with Mr. Ramirez, Justin turned once again to Dad. "I'm really sorry about those CDs, Dad, but—"

Dad interrupted again, this time with a big hug. "Justin, I know how bad you feel about this. You don't have to keep apologizing. . . ."

"I'm afraid it's not as easy as that," Mr. Ramirez broke in sternly. "Justin has been involved in a federal crime. We're going to need some explanations."

Justin swallowed hard. What kind of trouble was he in?

But Mr. Ramirez didn't appear too angry as he motioned them to sit on the sofa. He pulled an armchair closer and began, "Start at the beginning, Justin. Tell me exactly how you got involved with Grady O'Brian."

It took Justin a long time to tell his story. Mr. Ramirez scribbled notes in a small black notebook, interrupting often to demand more specific details. Dad tightened his arm around Justin's shoulders when he explained how Grady had threatened Dad's arrest to get Justin to work for him.

"Then, tonight when Mr. Ramirez said they'd traced the copies to your computer . . . Well, I knew I'd really gotten you into trouble! I figured they'd arrest you if I couldn't get Grady to say it was his idea."

"Justin, I was in no danger of being arrested," Dad broke in gently. "When the investigators checked with my secretary and the guard at the front gate, they found that I hadn't even been in the office at the time the computer logged those copies. But after they induced Miss Pettigrew to talk, they found out that *you* had been in my office. And since Mr. Ramirez had seen you with Grady, who was already under investigation . . . Well, they just put two and two together."

Justin felt like a fool. How could he have fallen for such lies?

Dad shook his head, "What I don't get is . . . how in the world did you ever figure out my password?"

Justin explained how he'd worked out the password and made the copies. "I'm sorry I lied to you, Dad. I . . . I thought I had to, but I know now that I was wrong."

"You're forgiven, Justin." Dad's eyes were fixed on him. "You thought you were helping me—and your country."

He cleared his throat. "But next time, son, give me credit for being a little harder to fool. And always remember—if an adult asks you to keep a secret from your parents, you can bet something's wrong. You come tell me right away!"

Justin nodded sheepishly and completed his story. Then Jenny explained her part in the evening's events. As she finished, Justin looked over at Mr. Ramirez. He felt stupid for assuming that Mr. Ramirez was an Arab terrorist just because of his similar coloring.

"I'm sorry I ran away from you," he told Mr. Ramirez. "I thought you were trying to steal the plans." Justin rubbed his eyes with his hands. "I was such an idiot! I believed everything Grady told me."

"Don't feel too badly," Mr. Ramirez answered with unexpected kindness. "Grady O'Brian has fooled a lot of older and more experienced heads than yours. The truth is, Grady *was* an NSA agent at one time. He was one of the best! I worked with him a couple of times when I first joined the agency, and I can tell you he could talk the head of the Russian KGB into turning over state secrets. But he decided there was more money on the other side of the law."

Mr. Ramirez slammed his notebook shut. "Grady used old military contacts from his Agency days to find out about the GP145. That's how he learned of a young computer genius who had been fired from the project for using his computer skills to steal classified information."

"Hacker!" exclaimed Justin.

Dad snapped his fingers. "That's where I've seen his face before. He wasn't in my department, or I'd have recognized him right off."

"Hacker wanted revenge *and* money!" Mr. Ramirez explained. "It was easy enough for Grady to talk him into pooling resources. The Arab Front for World Liberation had already offered Grady a hundred million dollars for the GP145. The plan was for Hacker to use his knowledge of the Boeing security system to break into the mainframe computer and steal the invisibility shield. But there had been too many changes in the system since Hacker left. Grady and Hacker needed help inside Boeing to get those plans. Justin was a piece of luck they hadn't expected."

Justin flushed red as the NSA agent turned his sharp gaze on him. Dad seemed to sense Justin's embarrassment and added, "Well, at least you saved the plans from falling into enemy hands, Justin. If you hadn't been there, Grady would have found another way to break into Boeing, and we might not have been able to stop him." Dad sighed as he added heavily, "I'll have to call my superiors and let them know that the GP145 is completely gone. The invisibility shield project is a total loss."

"But, Dad!" began Justin, this time without interruption. "That's what I've been trying to tell you. The plans *aren't* gone!"

"Maybe with enough time, we can duplicate . . ." Dad swiveled around to stare at his son. "What did you say, Justin?"

"I said, the plans *aren't* gone! When Grady asked me to make that copy—well, you always told me to make a backup, so I did." Justin looked at his father. "Then when I found out that all your files were destroyed, well . . . I didn't know if Grady was responsible. But I just couldn't give him the only copies left of the project. I mean, what if something happened to him? Besides, those were *your* plans. Anyway, I figured he only needed one copy."

Dad gripped Justin's shoulder tightly. "Are you telling me you have the other copy of those plans?"

Justin nodded. "I was afraid Mr. Ramirez here would find it if I left it in the house. Remember, I thought he was one of the bad guys, so . . ." Justin paused dramatically and caught his breath.

Jenny nudged him impatiently. "Come on, Justin! Where is it?" He shrugged nonchalantly, but his grin almost split his freckled cheeks. "I stuck it in the mail. Dad should get it tomorrow afternoon—that is, unless you want to break into the mailbox down near the ferry terminal. It should still be there. The next pickup is tomorrow morning."

The stunned reaction from Justin's audience was almost worth all the pain that had brought him to this point. The two men sat speechlessly staring. Then Jenny let out a war whoop. "Way to go, Justin!"

Mr. Ramirez leaned over and shook his hand. "Justin, that was brilliant! I take back all the things I thought about you these past few days when I was chasing you and Grady around the city." He rose to his feet and said, "Excuse me while I make a phone call. I think I have enough influence to get that mailbox opened tonight."

Mr. Ramirez flipped open his cellular phone and gave a few clipped orders. Then he turned back to the three Parkers. His sharp gaze softened as he seemed to take in for the first time Justin's still wet and torn clothing. His socks were shredded and what showed of his feet looked bruised and swollen.

"It's time we get you three home," said Mr. Ramirez. "Justin's been through more than enough for one night."

This time Justin enjoyed the boat ride across the Sound. He had borrowed one of the heavy winter coats from the ranger's house. Curled warm and snug next to Jenny in the cabin of the small boat, he watched sleepily as the pointed prow cut through the waves toward the glittering lights of Seattle. Justin was just dropping off to sleep when the electronic buzz of Mr. Ramirez' cell phone startled him awake.

"They located the CD," explained Mr. Ramirez. "They're already booting the material back into the Boeing computer. And it all seems to be there."

"Thank God!" Dad let out a war whoop just like Jenny's and grabbed Justin. "Son, I don't know how to thank you. You've done your country and Boeing an enormous service. Not to mention saving my job!"

"Would you have really lost your job if they hadn't gotten the plans back?" asked Jenny. "Even if it wasn't you who stole them?"

"Probably. Since it was my own son—and my password—that Grady used to break into the mainframe computer."

Justin was glad he hadn't known the risk to his father's job on top of everything else. But this wasn't the last revelation for the evening. When the three Parkers arrived back home, they were met by Mom at the front door. After some brief hugging and sincere scolding, Mom pulled Dad aside.

"Ron, you have a visitor," she whispered urgently. "He says you are expecting him."

"Abdul!" Dad slapped his forehead. "He's flying out tonight. I promised him a ride to the airport."

With long strides, he led the way inside. Abdul el Kutub was waiting for them in the living room. Looking exotic as ever in his flowing white robes and jeweled turban, he swept across the room to give Dad a smacking kiss on each cheek.

"Your wife told me there was trouble—great danger!" Abdul exclaimed throwing his hands up with horror. "I am so glad to see that you and your children are safe."

The Arab visitor turned to bow to Jenny, and Justin tugged on Dad's arm. "Dad, I've got to talk to you," he whispered. "It's about Abdul."

Dad glanced over at Abdul, who was paying Jenny an extravagant compliment, then back to Justin. "What is it, son?"

"It's just . . . there's something I still don't understand," Justin spoke in a low voice. "I know they said Abdul wasn't really a spy. But, well . . . I overheard you two down in the office. I was going to tell you about Grady then, but when you said that you really were passing information to Abdul . . ."

Dad looked completely puzzled. "Justin, you're going to have to start over. What exactly did you overhear?"

"You said you'd gotten the data from the Boeing computer."

Justin quickly repeated everything he could recall from that eavesdropped conversation. "You said you were going to work in his country—that you'd been keeping it a secret. You were afraid we'd be upset. . . . I thought . . ." —he finished lamely— "I don't know what I thought."

Justin was startled when Dad threw back his head and laughed, a hearty, booming laugh such as Justin hadn't heard from his father since this whole miserable mess had started. Embarrassed, he saw that Abdul and Jenny and Mom had turned around to stare.

Catching Justin's frown, Dad wiped his eyes. "I'm sorry, Justin. I know it isn't funny to you. And I can understand how you could have misinterpreted my words."

Still grinning, he explained, "The CDs I passed on to Abdul were completely authorized by Boeing. They just contained some unclassified technical information—engine specifications and airplane maintenance manuals. It's all part of our program to offer technical support to less-developed countries."

Dad smiled across at his Arab guest. "I met Abdul through this program. His father is a sheik who controls a large area of his country. The first time I met Abdul, I shared my faith in Jesus Christ with him. I helped him find an Arabic Bible, and he began to read and study it. Now, whenever he visits Seattle, he comes to me with more questions about the Christian faith."

Justin nodded. For the most part, it made sense. "But what about what you said about working in his country—and keeping it a secret?"

Dad chuckled. "Well, I guess it's time to let you and Jenny in on something your mother and I have been discussing." He motioned them all over to the chairs. "You know we have always been interested in missions. We've had missionaries in our home as often as possible, and we support several missionaries in different countries. But we've always dreamed of doing more."

Justin and Jenny both listened with wide-eyed interest. Dad continued explaining, "I'm no great preacher, but I've wondered if there was some way I could use my computer skills to serve God. Some months back, I had a chance to visit with a representative of a mission called Christian Technicians International—or CTI. It's a group of Christian electronic technicians who help missionaries and Christian relief organizations around the world to set up computer equipment and programs to assist in their ministries."

Dad glanced across at Abdul's big smile. "Then I met Abdul. In his country missionaries aren't allowed to preach the gospel. But Abdul has talked his father into allowing Christian doctors and nurses to come in to set up clinics and teach health care to his people. CTI technicians would set up the computers and equipment necessary. Abdul wanted me to be the one to come to his country."

Dad looked at Mom. "At first, I told Abdul that I couldn't go—not with my job and family responsibilities. But I started praying about it, and God began to open the doors. Boeing agreed to give me a six-month leave from my job. CTI accepted me to work with them—not just in Abdul's country, but anywhere they need help. I know how hard it has been for you two to get used to your new school this year. I didn't want to worry you with another change until there was a real possibility that we would go."

A twinkle crept into Dad's eyes as he looked from Justin to Jenny. "Well, kids? How do you feel about a few months on the other side of the Atlantic? It would mean studying by correspondence—since there wouldn't be any English-speaking schools. And I can't even say where we'll be from one week to the next—Saudi Arabia, Egypt, Israel, Russia—wherever we're needed. Would you be willing to go?"

Go! Exchanging excited glances, Justin and Jenny both burst out, "Of course we want to go!"

Jenny turned eagerly to Abdul. "Does this mean we'll be staying in your house? Will we meet your son and daughter—the ones that are our ages?"

"Enough!" Mom broke in, laughing. "You two are wet and cold." Her nose wrinkled as she looked over Justin's muddy clothing beneath the borrowed coat. "And filthy! You'd better get washed and changed before any further discussion."

Tired and dirty as he was, Justin obeyed reluctantly. He had a feeling that the babble of conversation breaking out behind him among the three adults meant more adventures ahead.

A camel caravan across the desert? The mysterious pyramids and temples of Egypt? Maybe even walking in Jesus' footsteps in the Old City of Jerusalem!

One exotic scene chased another through his mind as he headed down the hall. Africa, the Middle East—who cared where they went first? There was a whole exciting world just waiting out there!

PARKER TWINS' POWER

Don't Miss Any of These High Octane Adventures

Captured in Colombia

Cave of the Inca Re

Jungle Hideout

Mystery at Death Canyon

Race for the Secret Code

Secret of the Dragon Mark